THE DREAM THING

MOIRA ANDREW

The Dream Thing

First Edition: 2010

Published by:
Palores Publications,
11a Penryn Street, Redruth, Kernow TR15 2SP, UK.

Designed & Printed by:
The St Ives Printing & Publishing Company,
High Street, St Ives, Cornwall TR26 1RS, UK

ISBN 978 1 906845 14 8

THE DREAM THING

CHAPTER ONE

IT MUST HAVE been the dream-thing. It had been happening to her a lot recently, well, ever since she had discovered that Mum wasn't coming back. Not that she minded living with Dad. He was OK. Mostly.

Not much good at sewing on buttons, but then, neither was Mum, come to that. And there wasn't much call for button-sewing-on. Sticky tape did a perfectly good job, or safety pins, if you could find them. She gazed at the silver stars fixed to her bedroom ceiling. Some of them were coming off. If she could be bothered, she'd clamber up on the chest of drawers and glue them back. Then again, perhaps not, too much hassle. Even this early in the day, it was hot, too hot for anything energetic. She remembered Mum brimming with enthusiasm as she stuck them on, 'Your very own diamonds in the sky,' she'd said. She often came up with this kind of off-the-wall stuff.

Take her name, that had been another of Mum's wacky ideas. 'On the morning you were born,' – cue for one of her goofy grins – 'I looked out of the bedroom window and hundreds of golden marigolds smiled back at me, so I thought, Marigold, the perfect name for my baby.' (What Dad thought wasn't on record.) 'You smiled from the moment you were born, you know.' Mum got quite carried away with this story and the fact that she'd insisted on having her baby at home – all part of her touchy-feely mother-earth phase. It was quite probably rudbeckias she saw or tall buttercups, certainly yellow flowers of some kind. She wouldn't have known the difference. Just as well.

Marigold Merrick was bad enough. Imagine Rudbeckia Merrick! (If anything, Buttercup would have been even worse. Buttercup Merrick and she'd surely have done away with herself by now.) Doing away with herself. That was something Marigold thought about a lot.

She'd since found out, from her friend Jocelyn, who knew everything, that new babies never smile. That was something else her mother had got wrong. 'It's only wind that makes them look like they're smiling,' Jocelyn told her. So, if it hadn't been for a touch of wind, she might easily have had a proper name, she thought, like Sally or Jenny or Kylie or something perfectly ordinary.

Marigold felt rattled, the boy's stony-eyed stare still penetrating her imagination, taking some of the gloss off the morning. She got up and went to the window. She looked out at the untended garden, the lawn - well, more a minor jungle at this moment - a few straggly roses, some day-lilies, certainly no patch of bright marigolds smiling in the sun. Nothing there to take her mind off the pictures in her head. If she wasn't careful the dream-thing would come back to haunt her. She'd have to think about something else - and quick. That was part of the trouble, nobody knew who (or what) had begun to live inside her head. Not even Jocelyn. She'd have thought it gross.

Marigold moseyed on downstairs, counting the steps as she went. That was another important thing. Counting. She couldn't help it. She counted flagstones and railings, pots and pans, knickers and socks. Now socks, they posed a problem. Should she count them individually or in pairs?

The kitchen was its usual derelict Saturday morning self, dirty mugs, empty cat dishes, dried-on pizza plates in a forlorn heap by the sink. Marigold opened the fridge. There wasn't a lot there. Some cheese, a half-carton of orange juice, two out-of-date yogurts, three squashy tomatoes. No milk, so cereal wasn't an option. But what was that right at the back? A bar of dark chocolate, unopened. It was definitely her lucky day.

Dad must have left for work - he did occasionally take a tutor group on Saturdays. Or to go fishing. Or for a walk by the sea for some of his precious thinking time. She looked around for a note, but there wasn't one. This didn't surprise her. Sometimes Dad more or less forgot that she was there. She shrugged. It's how life was these days.

She grabbed the chocolate bar and tore open the wrapper, taste buds drooling in anticipation. She divided the chocolate into squares and counted them. Sixeen neat sections. Just the thing for an unhealthy breakfast. She found a newspaper, left ready to line the cat's box, so it must have been at least a week old. Not that it mattered. It was something to read. Marigold opened the back door and sat on the step, the paper on her knee, the chocolate laid out in a 4 times table pattern. It was shaping up to be an almost-perfect summer morning, she thought. Best of all, the dream-thing had all but disappeared.

It wasn't easy to remember what it was like before . . . before the dream-thing started big-time . . . before mum left . . . before they began to call her names. Fatty, Roly-Poly, Michelin Man – these were some of the kinder ones. Now it was Belly-Bulge, or worse Smelly Belly-Bulge. Just thinking about it inside her head, made Marigold shudder. And matters had been getting worse. It wasn't just name-calling these days. Now they had started doing things to her, like locking her in the toilet. She felt sick when she remembered how she had to be rescued half-in and half-out of the window, stuck fast like Pooh Bear. Still, today was Saturday. No need to worry about it until tomorrow night. Then a big fat worry, with school next day. And the dream-thing would be back, sure as eggs.

In the warmth of the morning, her mouth thick with the taste of chocolate, Marigold dared to re-run last night's dream-thing. Although the boy hadn't said much, as far as she could remember, he had watched her from behind a tree with that unblinking gaze of his, frightening her out of her wits. He wasn't a boy in the sense of a common-or-garden member of the male sex, but The Boy, pale and willowy with barely a hint of beard. It was his eyes that did it. Marigold had just to catch a glimpse of the sea on a sunny afternoon to wither inside herself. His eyes were blue stones, glittering like sun on water. They didn't move. They simply stared.

If she was caught off-guard and accidentally exchanged a glance with him, as you do in the normal way of things, Marigold was in his power. Being in thrall to The Boy scared her rigid. Sometimes she tried to keep awake all night, anything to thwart the dream-thing.

She finished her chocolate, screwed the wrapper into a knot and dusted herself down. She looked idly at the paper she'd been using as a tablecloth. It was full of last week's news. The recycling bag was the place for that. Not that she could find one, although its distinct blue plastic should have made it easy. When Mum had been around, recycling had been a big thing. Perhaps she should get more bags when she went to the shops. It would be the responsible thing to do. She smoothed the paper out ready for adding to the pile.

A blurry photograph, almost obscured by a smear of dried-on chocolate, but it was *him*, she was sure – same piercing eyes, white-blonde hair, slim build. The Boy. Her heart thumped with a steam-hammer beat. She read quickly through the short paragraph that went with it.

Luke Appleton, 15, missing from Cannington Children's Home. He has not been seen for several weeks. Both the home's house-parents and the police are very concerned for his welfare. Luke is fair, tall for his age with distinctive blue eyes. His birth-mother has been contacted, but she has no knowledge of his whereabouts. Can you help?

Marigold tore the article from the paper and stuffed it into the back pocket of her jeans. What she intended to do with it she had no idea. She could hardly go to the police and say that The Boy – Luke she supposed she should call him now – visited her in her dreams. First things first, she thought, putting the dishes to soak in the washing-up bowl. Then a trip to the Spar shop was called for before she and her father starved to death. She raided the emergency money-tin and sauntered out into the sunshine, surprised to find that it was already mid-day. Where had her morning gone?

She should walk more, she knew, jog even, to get rid of the bulge round her waist – perhaps tomorrow would be a good day to start. Marigold was a strong swimmer, or had been, but nowadays there wasn't time, what with her and Dad on their own – and they'd closed the local pool. Well, that was her excuse. If she was being truthful, she wouldn't be seen dead in a swimming costume, not until she'd lost a bit of weight. Mum might have bothered, maybe taken her to the new St Ives pool in the car. Not Dad, first he said, he didn't have the time, (not entirely accurate, Marigold thought) and second, he liked her cuddly, so why bother with exercise? 'I've no time for these skinny women you can't get a grip on,' he said.

She pulled her hoodie top down to disguise the spare tyre. But she couldn't stick it for long. It was much too hot to be wearing a fleece. So she gave in, unzipped it and tied it round her waist. It was the best she could do.

'Hey Goldielocks!' – a voice from the other side of the road. She ignored it and walked on, quickening her step. Ignore it, just ignore it, she told herself. She hadn't expected the name-calling lark to leak into her Saturday. She reached the tree-lined street down to the shops. 'Twenty-two, twenty-three, twenty-four . . .' under her breath. Seven more trees and she'd have made it to Spar. There was an order, a certain safety, about numbers.

'Goldielocks!' This time, she looked round. No-one from school, in fact no-one at all. The sun-yellowed street was empty, apart from an abandoned two-wheeler with stabilizers and an upturned doll's pram. Just her over-active imagination, she reassured herself – but worse, she'd lost count. That made her edgy.

'Don't your ears work today?' Not any old boy, but The Boy. He slouched alongside and reached for her elbow. 'Just say hello, go on.' She felt rooted to the spot with fear. What on earth was he doing out of dream-time?

'Gerroff,' she growled. 'Leave me alone.'

'It's me,' the boy persisted, staring at her with stony eyes.

'I've never seen you in my life before. Naff off – or I'll call the police!' Marigold felt bold – once she has passed the glass shop (she usually took time to gaze at the blue pots in the window, but not today), a gift boutique and the hairdresser's, she'd be within a few metres of the Spar shop.

'If that's the way you want to play it,' he shrugged, leaning against the shop door. 'I've all the time in the world. I'll wait.'

The shop was almost deserted, most people having better things to do with themselves on such a hot afternoon. Marigold took a wire basket. She picked up a wedge of Cheddar cheese, a half-litre of milk, a pack of sausages, a loaf. She tried to spin out the time she spent choosing. Her hand hovered over the sweets – Smarties, chocolate wafers, multi-packs of mini-bars.

'Not your best idea,' a voice from the shadowed doorway, 'that's if you're aiming to lose a bit of weight.'

A mind-reader on top of everything else! 'Get lost,' Marigold hissed, but for once, she by-passed the sweet shelf.

The boy was waiting for her. He stood up, stretched easily and followed her out into the street. 'Listen to me, Marigold, please just listen,' he said. She quickened her step, trying and failing to blank him out. He stepped in front of her, took her gently by the shoulders and turned her to face him. She could feel his rasping breath, the power of his menacing eyes. They stood there in the empty street, facing one another in silence. She waited for him to say something more.

Unexpectedly, he touched her cheek with his index finger. It was like a spider walking on her face. 'Nice skin,' he said. 'Like a gardenia petal.' It was the most complimentary thing anyone had ever said about her. She blushed, she couldn't help herself and felt a complete idiot.

'I love the touch of skin,' the boy mused. 'It's what I miss most.' Then quietly, pleading almost, 'Let me walk back up the hill with you.'

I'm seeing things. It's the dream-thing – in broad daylight – Marigold thought. 'OK,' she said, powerless as ever in his company. 'What d'you want?'

'To stay with you for a while – not long, I promise.'

'Well, you can't. Anyway, how do you know where I live? Have you been hanging around?'

'Sort of.'

Marigold shivered, despite the heat of the sun. Her fingers probed for the crumpled news item in her pocket. If only you knew, she thought. 'My dad would have a fit if he found out. He's a very private kind of man.'

'Don't tell him then. I won't be a problem, honestly. He won't even know I'm there. And I can keep an eye on you.'

She turned abruptly on the narrow pavement, nearly knocking the boy over. 'Keep an eye on *me?* Who do you think you are?' She began to walk away, but the boy followed, keeping a discreet distance behind her. Finally, curiosity got the better of her. Over her shoulder, she asked, 'Why me?'

'Because we're kind of friends already, come on, you know we are – and because you're going to need me one day.'

Marigold gathered her strength. 'Rubbish! I have never, repeat never, ever seen you in my life before.' Well, not in the light of day.

'If you believe that, you'll believe anything. Who do you think walks into your dreams at night? OK, not every night, I'll admit it, but a guy's got to have a night off now and again.' Out of breath by this time, Marigold didn't even try to reply. The boy fell into step beside her, taking the steep hill in his stride.

I hope Dad's at home, Marigold thought. The boy's nearness was beginning to get to her. She could smell the faint unwashed whiff of him, a smoky bonfire smell from his clothes. And she dared not look directly into his stony eyes. That would be too scary for words.

But Dad's car was nowhere in sight. She played for time. 'Give me a minute,' she said, putting her key into the lock, 'I'll need to check if my Dad's back yet.'

The boy stood close behind her, breathing on her neck. 'Come on, Goldielocks . . .'

'Marigold, to you.'

'Daft name. Anyway, you know very well your father isn't home.'

'How come?' Did he have telepathic powers on top of everything else?

'Easy. No car.' He gave her a bleak smile.

Marigold sighed and gave in. In a strange way she did feel as though she knew him. 'OK,' she said. She led the way into the kitchen. 'Sit down at the table and don't move.'

'You don't trust me, do you?' He sat, arms by his side, simply staring at her. A shadow fell across them. It was only a cloud passing over the sun, but it felt much more sinister.

'Why should I?' Marigold edged towards the sink. The knife drawer was under the worktop, if only she could reach in for the bread knife, she'd feel a lot safer.

The boy's cold gaze followed her. 'I wouldn't if I were you.' So he knew about the knife. She felt a shiver go up her spine. 'Anyway, nothing you do will make a lot of difference, so you might as well sit and talk to me.' Marigold, on automatic pilot, put the milk and cheese into the fridge, before choosing a chair as far away from the boy as possible. He leaned forward, elbows on the table, beginning to look almost at home.

Marigold poured herself a Coke. 'Want one?' She held out a can. He shook his head, pale eyes never leaving her face. It was completely unnerving, the dream-thing come true. If only there were things to count. She looked wildly round the kitchen, saw the pile of old newspapers and started counting under her breath.

Get a grip, Marigold told herself. Newspapers! It was now or never. 'Have you seen this?' she ventured, taking the scrap of paper from her jeans' pocket. She smoothed it out and passed it to the boy. 'Is this you? Luke? Luke Appleton?' She sounded dry and breathy, quite unlike her usual self.

The boy nodded, took the paper, read it slowly, mouthing the words under his breath. 'Birth-mother? But she's . . .' he muttered under his breath. Then, aloud, 'You know what local papers are like.

They never get their facts right . . .' He hesitated, alert to the sound of car tyres scrunching to a stop in the gravel outside.

'Dad!'

'I'd better disappear,' the boy said – and did. At least, it seemed like that to Marigold.

Her father burst through the back door with the chink of car keys and a deep throaty sigh. 'God, it's hot,' he said, flopping down in the very chair that the boy had been sitting on. 'Any chance of a cold beer, love?'

'Will a Coke do?' As usual, Marigold's dad seemed to expect the fridge to refill itself, without any effort on his part.

'I thought you might have made it to the Spar this morning,' he grumbled.

'I did, but beer wasn't on my list.' She tried not to sound put-upon, but failed.

'You mean I have to write everything down? You get more like your mother every day!' he said, downing the can of Coke in one long gulp.

'Miserable so-and-so,' a sotto-voce comment from the corner of the kitchen. Marigold spun round. No-one there. Not a flicker from Dad.

'But Dad, they're not supposed to sell me beer and stuff.'

'Hasn't stopped them before, has it? Well, I suppose I'll have to go down the pub instead. No rest for the wicked!' A quick tap on his daughter's shoulder and he was off, keys swinging from his fingers. Then, second thoughts getting the better of him, he put his head back round the door. 'Everything all right, love? Nothing you want?' Neither expecting nor waiting for a reply, he leapt into the car, put it in gear and reversed out into the road.

'Does he go on like that all the time?' the boy asked, materialising from the shadows.

'It's just his way,' Marigold said, feeling an absurd need to apologise. She wiped down the table, ran hot water into the bowl and began to wash up, counting the mugs and plates as she went, seven plates, eleven mugs. How had they managed that number between them? Without a word, the boy found a tea-towel and dried the dishes in a companionable kind of way. Where on earth do we go from here? Marigold wondered. If only Jocelyn were at home – she'd make her see sense – but she was a reluctant visitor to some long-lost auntie in Exeter this weekend. 'How long are you intending to stay?' she asked.

'Till the job's done, I imagine.' Marigold felt a surge of fright at the mention of a mysterious job, but didn't want to explore the idea further. The look in his eyes convinced her that she was somehow involved – and that was downright scary.

'And when will that be?'

He shrugged. 'Your guess is as good as mine.' End of conversation. The boy didn't seem to need to talk, to explain.

Marigold looked at her watch. Time dragged. She looked out of the window. The vivid summer afternoon had dimmed. 'The wind's coming up,' she said. The trees at the bottom of the garden were swaying, their leaves chattering in distress, the sky clouding over.

Luke eyed the lowering weather. 'There's a storm on the way. I'd close the windows, if I were you,' he suggested. 'Where is this pub then? Is it far?'

'At the other end of town. Dad shouldn't be long.' She considered his options. Realistically, he might be in any one of three or four pubs. Or perhaps he had made his way to St Ives itself. Sometimes he did this, not spying, of course. 'Just looking out for your mum,' he had said on occasion, justifying himself. Sometimes he chose not to say where he'd been. In which case, he might not be back until morning. She had no intention of sharing this information with the boy who was still gazing at her intently, stone-blue eyes glittering. She had to make Luke believe that her father had done no more than pop out, that he'd be home anytime soon.

Although it had become eerily dark, there was a strange green light in the sky, a sudden downpour of rain, black rods bouncing off the parched ground. Marigold curled deep into an armchair by the empty fireplace, knees up to her chin, feet tucked in. The cat jumped through the cat-door, shaking its soaking fur like a dog. He leapt on to Marigold's lap and she was glad of its reassuring deep-throated purr. 'You don't need to stay,' she said to Luke as she stroked the wet cat. 'I'm OK. Honestly.'

'Funny, you don't look it,' Luke said. 'Anyway, I have to stick around. I'm supposed to be looking after you.' He settled himself by the window, apparently mesmerised by the ferocity of the storm.

It was obvious that had no intention of leaving. Marigold sighed. 'You'd better tell me what it's all about,' she said.

The boy pulled up a chair and sat opposite her. 'Long story,' he said.

CHAPTER TWO

THE BOY HAD dressed quickly, shrugging into jeans and top, trainers and anorak. He took what the lads called the scenic route, swinging out of the window to shin down ivy twisted thick as a mooring rope, till he made it on to the lintel over the front door. Then a jump into the soft earth and he was off at a loping run.

It was a safe bet that he wouldn't be missed until the breakfast head count. Even then, his mate Danny was sure to say, 'Not to worry, you know what Luke's like, probably gone off on some mad project of his own.'

And Leslie, the house-father, would growl, 'Well, I hope he's not expecting me to hang around waiting for him. If he's late, he's late and he'll have to take what's coming to him.' Leslie had little time for either his charges or their problems.

He would have chewed his yellow moustache, chivvying the other four into the old estate car, no turning back for forgotten reading books or swimming kit, Radio 5 Live at top volume until he reached the school gates. 'See you all later, more's the pity,' he'd grumble and he'd be on his way, job done, all thoughts of his house-family wiped from his mind.

It was Helen's fault, Leslie concluded, going over in his mind, for at least the hundredth time, the route his life was taking. OK, so they'd been in a tight spot for money, but getting involved with a children's home was the last thing he had wanted.

He remembered Helen coming across an advert in the local paper. 'Come on, it's good money. Let's give it a try.' And he had been persuaded, much against his better judgment. Kids, who'd have 'em? That was Leslie's philosophy and the close-up reality hadn't changed his mind one bit. Helen could go on training courses till she was blue in the face, he had no intention of joining her. Who needs training to look after a bunch of kids? He stopped to pick up a paper, turned to the last page, made his selection and took his usual daily trip to the bookies'.

Then, footloose and fancy-free, he set off for the races. Soon neither wife, nor kids, either his own or anyone else's, would hold him back. He would make his fortune one of these days, he felt it in his water, and then there would be no stopping him. He pulled down the vanity mirror, smoothed his eyebrows with a bit of spit and dragged a comb through his thinning hair. That'll have to do, he thought, before losing himself in his favourite morning reverie.

First they'd ditch the kids, then just the two of them, off to the Bahamas or somewhere and a life in the sun. In fact, he might even go on his own, see how he felt about that later. He'd sure have a lot more fun that way. Birds, booze and constant sunshine, you couldn't beat it.

Day-dreaming, Leslie didn't see the boy slide out from behind the trees. He didn't see the stone until it ricocheted off the windscreen. By then it was too late.

The car veered off the road and smacked clean into the trunk of an ancient tree, the driver slumped against the steering wheel, blood pouring from a gash in his head where he had collided with the rearview mirror. Leslie didn't do seatbelts unless he saw a cop car on the horizon. Sissy stuff, he'd always thought. Although the bonnet had folded into itself on impact, the engine was still running. It sounded thunderously loud in the hushed clearing. Not that Leslie was aware of it – or anything else, for that matter.

The boy felt super-calm. Except for the Voice in his head, he was in charge of his fate for the very first time he could remember. He reached into the car, edged past Leslie's inert body and switched off the engine. Only the trickle of blood gave the game away. Apart from that, you'd have thought he was asleep. At least, he had prevented the whole thing from going up in flames, the boy thought, pocketing the key. True the house father was a thug at heart, but even he didn't deserve that kind of fate. Not that Luke could take all the credit, of course, the Voice had suggested it first.

Luke knew himself to be a misfit, a loner, totally unsuited for the communal life of a care home, even had it been a topnotch institution which *Cannington* certainly wasn't. But you didn't get a lot of choice in this kind of thing. It wasn't like choosing a holiday airline or the best value supermarket – you just had to go where you were sent. And he'd been sent to *Cannington,* into the rough and ready care of Helen and Leslie Henderson.

The other kids didn't seem to mind so much. They just got on with things, played with friends, moaned a bit – Danny even made jokes, in a Tracey Beaker kind of way. Not him. He needed to be on his own a lot of the time. He needed to look at things, to sort them out in his head, to think. And he needed time to listen to the Voice. The others thought he was a weirdo.

Maybe he was. Even when he'd been a little kid at home in their flat in downtown Bristol, he didn't seem to fit in and his mother hadn't known what to do with him half the time. 'You'll come to a sticky end one of these days,' she'd say. 'Well, don't say I didn't warn you.'

He seldom argued back, just stared at her in silence, blue eyes wide and still. 'And don't look at me like that, child. You'll scare the living daylights out of me!' and she'd aim a slap at his legs. Then she'd be off down the boozer or wherever she went, out of her head most of the time. Mostly he lived at Gran's house, just a couple of doors away. If only Gran had been his mum, things might have been different.

Even she sometimes said he must have been wished on the family by a bad fairy. 'A fairy put a spell on that boy at birth,' she used to say, 'those eyes . . .' but she said it with a smile in her voice. And she'd hug him hard, so that he knew she didn't really mean it. In fact, he was the apple of her eye, so she said, and he'd have a picture of her with apples where her eyes should be. But she was always saying odd unexpected things that set him thinking. That was one of the reasons why he loved her so much. Then one day Gran died. She didn't fall, she wasn't ill, she just wasn't there any more.

He simply hadn't expected Gran to die. Other grandmothers died from time to time, he knew that. But not his. He thought about her veined cheeks, her floury hands, her way with cinnamon pie. He couldn't believe he'd never hear her laugh again, that whispery papery laugh that was all her own. He couldn't believe she'd vanished the way dead people do, leaving nothing of herself behind, neither the faint whiff of lavender, nor the soft spongy feel of her arms. It left him feeling empty inside, and worse – there was no escape, nowhere for him to go.

He'd stayed around Mum's flat for a while, but the rent didn't get paid and they turned off the electrics and the water. Then his mother got beaten up and disappeared – into one of those women's shelters, they told him, although he had since privately decided that she was dead. If Gran could up and die, why not Mum?

He didn't go to school much after that. He roamed the woods by the Downs, looking at birds and squirrels and fish – and listening to the Voice in his head, even louder and more insistent now than it used to be. In some ways, the Voice had become a kind of best mate. He spent occasional days loafing about the streets nicking stuff, nothing expensive, just enough to keep body and soul together. Until he got caught, that is.

That was when the jaws of the care home snapped shut. He was only a kid at the time, badly behaved and barely able to read. But he was a thinker. He thought a lot about things; where had Gran gone when she died? – it couldn't be heaven, he figured, the place must be full to bursting if every dead person went there – what was beyond black holes? what went on in other people's heads? what was his mum doing now? – if she was still around – what would become of him when grew up? that kind of thing. And why he appeared so strange to other people? Was it just his eyes that did it?

He scooped out a hollow for himself among the fallen leaves and stretched out. He heard the river gurgling over stones, trees gossiping in the breeze, animals scuttering in the undergrowth and, in the distance, cars hurtling along the road. He heard a police car arrive, doors opening, muted voices muttering into radios. He was so well hidden and kept so still that no-one was aware of his presence.

The boy felt that Leslie's drama had absolutely nothing to do with him. It was as though there was a pane of glass between him and the crashed car. He settled down to think. Thinking time was scarce in the Home, but for once there was nobody chasing him to do something useful, like clearing the dining tables or looking after the little ones or doing his homework. That was how life was at *Cannington,* never an idle moment.

Things hadn't always been so tough. He remembered how it had been when he'd been very little, not much more than a baby, just Mum and him at home, Gran down the street. Mostly they'd been happy. When Mum was in the money she was always buying him things; an electric car that was thrown out when the battery went dead, a bright orange yo-yo, bags of sweets – and once, when he was about six, a second-hand book of poems. Not that the words made a lot of sense to him, but he loved the lavish illustrations, the jewelled colours, the intricate patterns. It was his favourite present ever.

One day, he took the well-thumbed book to school, but the boys laughed and the teacher asked sarcastically when he was going to learn to read it for himself. So he didn't dare bring it in again. Where did it get to? he wondered. He wished he could have another look at it, just this one last time, especially now his reading had gone up a notch. He was still in the bottom group, but he could just about keep up.

He remembered how sometimes his mother used to let him sleep in her bed. She didn't have Gran's lavender smell, but she usually had a faint flowery smell about her, when she hadn't been drinking, that is. She used to let him touch her skin. He found that his fingers had memorised how it felt to stroke her cheeks, trail along her arms, even down the length of her body sometimes. Now that was special and he shivered, remembering.

Then he heard the nee-naw of an ambulance and the voices of paramedics going about their business. The police must have directed them to Leslie's car. In a way he hoped he hadn't been too badly hurt. He wasn't the world's best house-father, but Luke didn't want a major injury, or worse, a murder, on his conscience. In fact, even if the Voice hadn't prompted him, he'd have dialled 999 himself.

He glanced at his watch. No-one would begin to worry about him until somewhere around five when they discovered he hadn't been to school. Or perhaps everyone was too busy worrying about Leslie to bother. After all, he had been known to go walkabout before.

But this time things were different, not that anyone else knew, of course. This time he had to make choices. Would it be the Clifton Suspension Bridge? That would mean getting back to Bristol, too risky. Multi-storey car park? The sea? He didn't think he'd have the bottle for jumping, so perhaps a stroll into the waves would be the best bet. That meant getting to the seaside, anywhere in Cornwall would do. He consulted a map in his head, realised that it would mean a journey by train. Or bus? Another decision - whatever. In the meantime, he lay soaking up the sun, arms behind his head. That was another thing to think about, what being dead was like. Well, he'd soon find out.

'So which did you choose?' Marigold asked. She was huddled in a chair by the empty fireplace. The garden, drenched now, looked even more uninviting than it had earlier that day, straggly flowers bowed down, their colours dimmed. She was reluctantly beginning to accept the boy's presence. He was someone to talk to, interesting even, if a tad on the weird side. And, of course, she too had occasionally thought about ways of finishing herself off – well, not very seriously, truth to tell. Here, sitting on the edge of the kitchen table, swinging his legs like a metronome, was someone who had actually done it.

The boy was silent. He did that strange thing with his eyes, staring at nothing, that she'd got used to in the dream-thing. 'Did you go for drowning, then?' Marigold persisted. She couldn't imagine doing it that way, she loved the water too much – and anyway, she was possibly too good a swimmer to drown.

'Well, I didn't get to choose in the end,' he said, almost smiling at some picture he'd built up inside his head.

He had waited where he was until it began to get dark. Hunger growled in his stomach, after all he'd had nothing much to eat all day, an apple, a bar of chocolate and a packet of cheese and onion crisps, not his flavour of choice, but then again, beggars (or more accurately, petty thieves) can't be choosers. He grinned to think how true this was. The cheese and onion had been the nearest at the petrol station check-out as the attendant fiddled with change for a senior citizen. He wouldn't have chosen Turkish Delight either, come to think. But it had filled a gap. Now, however, he felt the need for something more substantial.

Nothing else for it, he'd have to leave his woodland cocoon. Anyway, it had gone cool. Soon it would be too cold to lie around in comfort. He heaved himself up, dusted off his anorak and made sure that he hadn't left empty cans and wrappers. You couldn't be too careful about things like that, he thought, what with DNA and stuff.

The Voice had decreed that water was the way to go, so he decided to make for the bus station in Bodmin. There was sure to be a bus going towards the sea, Falmouth, Penzance, anywhere – he'd take a chance when he got there. Making every effort to empty his head, he trudged along, glad that he'd come to a decision at last, well, if he didn't duck out at the last minute.

He was so preoccupied that he barely noticed the Neddie Allthorpe lorry slowing to a stop beside him.

'Looking for a lift?' the man asked. 'Jump up.'

'Thanks.'

The driver looked the boy over, only a thin anorak, no rucksack. 'Leaving home?' he asked.

'Sort of.'

'It's OK. You don't have to talk if you don't want to.' The driver concentrated as he drove off. 'Did it myself once when I was a lad. Sometimes a guy's gotta do what a guy's gotta do, yeah?'

'Yeah.' The boy's head was getting crowded. Not only the Voice, but now the friendly driver as well. He stared straight ahead, unable to string the words of a simple conversation together.

The lorry driver tried again. 'Hungry?' He produced a pack of mangled sausage rolls from between the front seats.

'Not one of them veggies, are you?'

He shook his head, managed another 'Thanks,' and began to devour the sausage roll, more greasy pastry than meat.

'Drink?' From some mysterious hiding place the driver brought out two cans of lager. 'Not supposed to when I'm driving, but one won't hurt, what d'you say?'

They settled into a fairly comfortable silence. Night came slowly, grey and unsubstantial at first, cars and lorries prodding the dimming day with thin pencils of light. Suddenly it was truly dark and the yellow headlights brightened, dazzling his eyes. They stopped for a roadside pee and the driver unpopped a second can of lager.

'You?' he asked. The boy shook his head.

'Is it far?' he asked. 'To the sea?'

'It's a bit late for a swim, isn't it? Shouldn't be more than an hour at most.' He threw the empty can over the hedge. 'Better be getting on then.' And they climbed back up into the fuggy cab. The boy, when he'd found out where they were heading, had spun him a tale about an elderly grandmother who lived near Falmouth. 'She's got an old dog that needs walking, so I'm going to stay with her for a day or two,' he had said.

The driver didn't believe a word of it, but it was none of his business and the lad was a bit of company, even although he didn't talk much. He yawned, thinking that perhaps he shouldn't have had that second drink, turned the music up and put his foot down. If he got a move on, he'd just make 'The Spotted Cow' before closing. In the dark, he thought about the girl behind the bar, and grinned to himself in anticipation.

A tight bend, a narrow bridge and an oncoming car. The driver slammed on the brakes, but too late.

'So I didn't get a choice,' the boy said. 'Drowned, just like the Voice said.'

'What voice?'

'The one in my head. Don't you have a Voice?'

'No, not exactly.' Did the dream-thing count? she wondered.

'It was all over in minutes. The lorry spun off the bridge and into the river. I vaguely remember the cabin filling up and me hanging upside down in the seat-belt, spluttering in the water, before I lost consciousness. Oh yes, they carted me off to the hospital and we had all that high-tech stuff you see on *Holby City*, but it didn't work. So here I am, kind of half-dead.'

'Come off it. You're either dead or you're not.'

'That's what I thought. But apparently there's a kind of halfway house if you get there before your time.'

'D'you mean you're too young or something?' Marigold felt a tinge of pity for the boy. He had a lost look, a bit like a puppy she and her mum had once found wandering on the beach. Wondering how much he should tell her, he looked away, searching for the right words.

'They sent me to look after you for a bit,' he said.

What an arrogant so-and-so, she thought, instantly forgetting to feel sorry for him. 'I can look after myself, thank you.' She flounced over to the window and stared at the grey rain, determined not to get involved any further, but the boy's incredible story had intrigued her. 'You mean you're a kind of angel?'

'I suppose.'

'Show me your wings then,' she said. 'Bet you haven't got any.'

'Course I haven't. Wings are out of fashion these days.'

Marigold twiddled the blind cord between her fingers. She thought about Luke's rambling story. 'Know something? You're nothing but a weirdo,' she said. 'I don't believe a word you say.' True, he had done the ghost-thing of disappearing into thin air when Dad arrived on the scene, but an angel? That was too much.

The boy got to his feet and stood like a shadow behind her. He wanted to stroke her bare brown arms, the way he had once done with his mother. But he guessed she'd have none of it and pushed his hands deep into his pockets, so he wouldn't be tempted. A crumpled tissue, a piece of string and right at the bottom, a key. Leslie's ignition key. He held it up.

'Believe me now?' he asked.

CHAPTER THREE

'HUH. THAT DOESN'T prove a thing,' Marigold said.

'I suppose not.' Luke sounded disappointed. He eased his backside on to the kitchen table, looking beyond the girl to some mysterious world of his own.

Marigold looked at his closed-down face, unsure how to respond. Her thoughts went back over his story. A day-dream? An angel? Some angel, throwing a stone at a car windscreen! More of a vandal, she decided.

'Who did you say he was? House-father or something? You didn't actually go away and leave the poor guy for dead?'

'Course, I didn't – I waited till I heard the ambulance arrive. What do you take me for?'

'That's the trouble. I don't know a thing about you – and I don't expect dreams count.'

'To tell the truth, I hardly recognise myself these days.' The rain began to ease off and a watery sun made a brave appearance. 'I'm stuck in limbo, you know, not quite here, not quite there.'

'Not all there, that's for sure!' Marigold tried a feeble giggle.

Luke simply glared, nailing her to the spot with those strange eyes of his. She wanted – needed – to know what made him tick, especially if he intended to hang around for much longer.

She tore her gaze away from his and looked out on to the sodden garden, talking back over her shoulder. 'How long have you been into this dream business?' she asked. No reply. 'Don't you want to talk about it?' Obviously not, she thought, and the silence between them lengthened.

Luke twirled the car key around by its fob. Then he said, 'Look at this – a lucky horse-shoe! Maybe that's what saved old Leslie.'

'It certainly didn't do much for you. What about the lorry driver? Is he . . .?'

'Dead? The lorry driver? No, he managed to get free . . . tried to haul me out too, but there was no way. I had it coming – the Voice said so.' Another cold hard stare.

'So what's it like – drowning, I mean? Does your whole life flash in front of your eyes like people say?'

'Sort of. There I was thrashing about in the water and I thought I saw my Gran looking down at me from an upstairs window and kind of shooing me away. And my mum, of course, I couldn't miss her. First I got a whiff of her perfume, mixed with cigarettes and booze, of course, and there she was stood beside me. She didn't look any different – streaky blonde hair, springy curls, untameable, just like she used to say. I could have reached out and touched her. But when I called her name, she pretended she didn't know me and I thought, so what's new?'

'Well, according to the paper, she hasn't forgotten you. What does it say?' Luke had shoved it under his jacket when he did his disappearing trick. Marigold didn't know how these things worked, but hoped that the article had re-appeared along with Luke himself. It had. Good. He reluctantly passed it over. 'Listen, it says, *'His birth-mother has been contacted, but she has no knowledge of his whereabouts.''*

'They always get things wrong. I guess my mother's dead, even deader than me.' He gave one of his wintry smiles, quite pleased with his attempt at a joke.

'She can't be, not if she's given an interview to the *Packet* – or to the police, whoever.'

'Told you, they always get things wrong. But I wish I knew – what if they're right this time? Maybe I should try to find her. Maybe she wasn't telling me to push off. I simply don't know what to do for the best.' He slumped down, head on his arms.

Marigold's eyes lit up. She had a project. This deadly weekend might yet be livened up. 'Cracked it!' she said. 'We could find out what's happened to your mum.'

'It's not as easy as that. We can hardly go down to the newspaper office and demand an interview. So where do you suggest we start, Smartypants?'

'Obvious. Ever heard of the internet?'

'I used to be a bit of an IT whiz-kid, although I say it myself. Are you online?' he looked around the kitchen. 'Through here?'

'No such luck. I use the library . . .'

'Don't people watch what you're up to?'

'Everybody's too involved in their own thing to bother. Anyway, we've got a good excuse, family-tree research. Are you up for it?'

'But what about your dad?'

'Oh, I'll leave him a note. He's used to that,' Marigold said airily. 'Let's go.'

Marigold snatched up her jacket, pocketed a couple of Kit-Kats and nipped into the loo. She emptied the rest of the emergency money into her purse. This could be classed as an emergency, she reckoned.

'The loo's at the end of the hall,' she said to Luke, pointing.

'Never need to use one these days,' he said. 'There's something to be said for almost-deadness, I suppose.'

They made their way down the road, skirting puddles as they went. Luke began to lag behind. 'Is it much further?' he asked. 'I don't seem to be built for serious walking at the moment. This is where wings might come in handy, I suppose.'

'But they'd make you look so uncool, wouldn't they?' Marigold teased.

Luke grinned back, his eyes losing some of their usual wariness. 'Point me in the right direction and I'll meet you at the door,' he said. Hot and bothered by this time – after all she'd been to Spar and back once already this afternoon – Marigold glared at him. Well, not at him exactly. The road was deserted.

'Luke?' she called. 'Where are you?' Not a sound. Nothing, just a silver sea glittering in the distance and a few picture-postcard yachts rocking at anchor. Puffed out, she laid her jacket on the damp grass verge and flopped down. If he can't be bothered to leg it to the library, neither would she. Two can play at the same game, she thought.

Come to think of it, this was the kind of stuff he got up to inside the dream-thing sometimes, coming and going to an internal timetable of his own. She unwrapped one of the biscuits. She had to keep her energy up somehow. The first crispy sugar boost went straight into her bloodstream and she began to feel better about Luke's sudden disappearance. She decided to wait it out. Either he'd come back to find her – or he wouldn't. She pretended she didn't care.

'Hey, look who's here? Batty Fatty Merrick, all on her own. Diddums!' Shadows crowded in around her as three of the Year 8s, a notorious bunch of bullies, appeared out of nowhere. A fist knocked the Kit-Kat from her hand and a trainer ground it into the mud.

'You shouldn't be noshing on chocolate biscuits – not with a fat belly like yours!'

'We're only doing this for your own good, you know. Got any more stashed away?' The ringleader had her on her back now, grabbing at her jacket pockets, tearing at her jeans. He found the second biscuit, ground it underfoot and waved the sticky mess triumphantly in front of her nose. 'Smell that,' he jeered. 'Chocolate! Yummy! I bet you'd die for it!' Marigold was terrified, too stunned to yell out. She curled into a ball, hoping against hope that they'd had their fun. That they'd go away. It's what usually happened.

She heard the jeering give way to an indignant curse and a yelp of pain. Squinting at the yobs from under a protective arm, she found the main man, Kevin Jenkins, sprawled on the footpath. 'What d'you want to do that for?' he demanded of the other two.

'Don't blame me! It was her, the silly bitch,' the smallest lad said accusingly.

'I'll soon wipe the grin off her fat face.' Kevin got up from the floor and lunged at her, fists flying.

Marigold might be overweight, but she was up in no time and fast on her feet, 'Get lost, you lot!' she shouted with a touch of her usual spirit and ran full tilt into Luke, who had suddenly materialised. He steadied her, meanwhile treating the three bullies to one of his best drop-dead stares.

'Hey look, Fatty's got a boyfriend! Fatty's got a boyfriend!' Afraid of losing face, the ringleader, squared up to Luke who neither moved nor said a word. Kevin's punch simply did not connect. It was like beating up a shadow. The sheer momentum pitched him forward on to his face. His mates stood watching as he picked himself up, trying to figure out what - or who - had floored him.

He dusted himself down, all bluster. 'What the hell happened?'

Unwilling to credit Marigold's wimpish boyfriend with a killer punch, the trio tried to put the blame on one another. Finally, they retreated up the road, mouthing 'Weirdo!' in an attempt to satisfy their bruised egos.

'You OK?' Luke asked.

'Well, we've lost our afternoon snack,' Marigold said. 'Otherwise, I'm more or less in one piece. How on earth did you manage that?'

'It wasn't difficult. I just stuck my foot out and he tripped over it. Invisibility has its compensations. I told you I'd been sent to look after you - I'm simply following instructions.'

'Thanks,' Marigold muttered.

'No problem. Hey, we'd better get to the library. It closes in half an hour. I saw the times on the door while I was waiting. What kept you?'

'What did you expect? You disappeared without a word. I thought I must be back inside the dream or wherever you hang out – that was, until you saw off the Y8 yobs.' She couldn't help smiling at the picture of their undignified downfall.

Although keeping pace with one another, neither felt the need to talk. Glancing at her companion from time to time, Marigold tried to make sense of what she'd seen. He looked so solid, proper flesh and bone, but she had definitely witnessed the yob's fist go right through him. Weird wasn't the word for him. He steered her up the library steps. The touch of his hand on her back was reassuringly warm.

The library assistant directed them to the computer bay. 'It's full at the moment, but if you can wait, one might become available before closing time.' She yawned and looked at her watch.

'What do you think?' Marigold asked – to fresh air.

'Sorry,' the woman said. 'You said . . . ?'

'Thanks, we'll – I'll wait.' Marigold realised that she'd have to get used to Luke's irritating disappearances. 'Where are you?' she whispered under her breath. No reply.

She gazed around the room at people flicking through books, replacing them on the shelves, tiptoeing to the desk. She glanced up at a row of dreary oil-paintings of long-dead benefactors. One moved, she was sure of it. Fascinated, she stared harder at the ancient guy in Mayor's fancy red robes and some kind of furry collar. He very deliberately held up the fingers of one hand and waggled them in her direction. She sniggered. The book-browsers glared. She looked again, this time the old man's five fingers were splayed out. Marigold nodded, it was Luke's idea of a joke. Did it mean that he'd wait for five minutes? Or what?

One of the computers became free. Marigold sat in front of it. She'd have to google, she knew, but what kind of questions should she ask? Then she found her fingers flicking across the keys of their own volition. Luke, she supposed.

'Five minutes to closing. Please shut down the computers.'

'But we haven't got anywhere,' Marigold said aloud.

'Not to worry. I'll kip down here. See you later.' Luke said, in a hoarse whisper. Nobody else as much as twitched.

'Please close down now!' the librarian sang out. She wanted to get on home – that much was obvious. She didn't approve of working on a Saturday afternoon, a fine sunny one, at that, now the rain had blown over. Marigold slouched against the desk, reluctant to give up so soon. Then she found herself being propelled towards the door.

'Go on,' Luke's voice hissed in her ear. 'I'll get down to a bit of research after everyone's gone. Oh, and give me a bell if the Y8 bullies are in a mood to beat you up again.'

'That's a fat lot of good if you're here and I'm there.'

'Get going, Goldielocks. We undead have our little ways . . . You'll see.'

When Marigold reached home, she was surprised to see her father's car in the drive.

As soon as she opened the door, Dad greeted her with, 'Where have you been, Kid? This is a fine time to get home.'

That's a turn-up for the books, she thought, saying as she flopped on to a chair, 'The library – that OK with you?'

'You might have said, I've been worried stiff.'

'Come on, Dad. I left you a note.' She unstuck the Post-it from the fridge door and waved it in front of his face. 'I bet you haven't read it. Anyway, it's only half past five, not the middle of the night . . .'

'Well, we haven't time to sit around arguing. We're off out you and me – about time we treated ourselves.'

'Out? Have we come into money then?'

'I don't know what to think about you, girl, always harping on about cash – you get more like your mother every day.'

'Not surprising, is it?' Marigold murmured under her breath.

'Come on, love. Get yourself prettied up for your old dad.' There was an unfamiliar wheedling tone in his voice.

'Dad, you know I don't do pretty,' she objected.

'Well, you do tonight. Go on, at least change into something clean.' She looked at him more closely – crisp open-neck shirt, slicked-back hair. She sniffed his chin. After-shave. He must be out to impress.

'Do me a favour and get a move on, Kiddo.' He glanced at his watch. 'I've booked us a table.'

Mollified, she said, 'OK, OK, whatever . . .' and went slowly upstairs to see if she had anything presentable to wear. She tipped tops out of drawers, tore trousers off hangers, even looked in the laundry basket. Everything she came across was too tight, faded or minus a button. Finally she settled on a blue shirt that gaped a bit and a gypsy-type skirt that Mum had left behind. Fortunately it had an elastic waist. Not the coolest outfit, but it would have to do.

'Come on, girl. At this rate it'll be breakfast time before we get out of here.' Dad opened the front door and stood at the bottom of the stairs, twiddling his car keys. He was beginning to lose patience, she could tell. When finally he shouted, 'Marigold, get down here *now!'* she knew he meant business.

Marigold's hair was her crowning glory. Everyone said so. Pity she hadn't had time to wash it. She dragged a brush through her curls and hoped for the best. It would have to do. She tumbled downstairs.

'Where are we going?' she asked as she settled breathless into the passenger seat. 'And why the hurry?'

'I'd like you to meet a friend of mine.'

'From work?' Dad nodded, eyes on the road ahead.

He taught surveying in a further education college in Redruth, but rarely talked about his colleagues and hadn't, to Marigold's knowledge, done much socialising since Mum disappeared, although there was no knowing who he hung out with when he went to the pub. He sounded so shifty that she was instantly suspicious. 'Like who?'

'Oh no-one you'd know. But I hope you'll like her.'

'Her?'

'Yes, her – anything wrong with that?'

'No, not really.' Marigold hesitated, 'What about Mum?' she asked.

'Nothing to do with your mother – nothing at all,' Dad said, his firm tone allowing no further comment.

The two went quiet, neither quite knowing what to say next. When they stopped at the lights, Dad flicked on the right-hand indicator. Truro then, he must really be in the money, she thought.

'Raining again,' he said finally, more to break an uncomfortable silence than an attempt at conversation. 'Mmm,' Marigold agreed. For a few minutes, there was only the squeaking of windscreen wipers and the sound of tyres squelching through puddles on the road. Then they both broke the silence together, 'For heaven's sake, try to be polite and don't argue the toss,' Dad said.

Marigold asked, 'What's her name?'

'Bunny.'

'Bunny? Nobody in the whole world's called Bunny!' She stifled a giggle.

'Well, not many people are called Marigold after all.'

'S'pose not.'

Another silence. 'How much further?'

'Ten minutes or so. We've been invited to Bunny's apartment for drinks first,' Dad said. Marigold's imagination went into total spin. How many fishing trips had been evenings out with Bunny? she wondered. What would she look like? Like Mum – perhaps not? In addition, she had to adjust to the idea of Dad as someone's boyfriend. Even her vivid imagination couldn't cope with the thought of Dad as boyfriend material, although with his mane of grey hair and his crinkly smile, he wasn't bad-looking, she supposed, for his age. It's bad enough to think of your parents *doing it,* but Dad getting horny with a strange woman. Impossible! Marigold closed her eyes.

'Calm down, Goldielocks. We're in this together,' a familiar whisper in her ear. She twisted round, delighted for once to glimpse the boy hovering over the back seat. 'Maybe it's not what you think. Perhaps they're just good friends.'

But no, they were obviously much more than that. They embraced as though they were trying to devour one another, kissing, kissing, his hands in her hair, on her hips. Once they had unpeeled themselves, Bunny swooped down on Marigold. 'And this is your lovely daughter, Ollie,' she said – Ollie? Her dad had never been Ollie in his life. Oliver mostly, Ol occasionally, never ever Ollie.

Marigold tried to shake hands, but was grasped by bony arms, jangling with silver bracelets and air-kissed three times. Then Bunny put her hands on Marigold's shoulders and pushed her an arm's-length away. 'Great hair, nice eyes – all is not lost,' she said, scrutinising her closely. 'We need to do some serious shopping, you and me.' It was all very arch and girly-girly. The trouble was, Marigold didn't do girly stuff – and it showed.

'I don't think my dad can afford much serious shopping right now,' she said, making it sound akin to baby-snatching. She perched on the edge of a pale cream sofa, scowling quietly to herself.

'Drinks?' Bunny asked. 'Your usual, Ollie? What about you, my dear?'

'I'll have what my dad's having,' Marigold said.

Bunny raised her eyebrows. 'I think you're rather young for G&T, don't you?'

'Well, you asked.' She knew she was being rude, but she didn't care. Dad looked daggers at her. 'Sorry,' she said. 'May I have a glass of water?'

'Still or sparkling?' Bunny was the perfect hostess.

Marigold wandered round the room, feigning an interest in the minimalist pictures on the walls – not entirely to her taste – but anything was better than watching her father play lover-boy. Bunny's apartment was the height of chic. From the acres of light wood flooring and elegant lampshades to the single vase of lilies placed just so on a glass table, Bunny's place was a million miles from their own cramped little house.

It was situated bang in the middle of Truro, beside the river. From the top-storey window, Marigold could see the trio of Cathedral spires, a maze of streets and the secretive river below. How could someone who worked in further education afford a pad like this? Dad was always complaining about the miserable salary they received.

Marigold didn't dare put her glass down on the living-room's glossy surfaces, so she wandered into the adjoining kitchen. It looked as though it had never been used, no half-opened packets, no nearly-new jars, no past-its-best fruit, just shiny chrome fittings and empty black worktops. Not exactly empty, she realised. Luke sat on top of the fridge, trainers tapping to some internal rhythm of his own.

'Shh, they'll hear you,' she hissed.

'Not a chance! They wouldn't hear a bomb going off.' He jerked his head towards the lounge. 'Cast your eyeballs over that!'

Sure enough, when she looked through the archway, she saw Bunny and her father wound around one another like a pair of amorous snakes, oblivious to everyone and everything – even snogging with tongues! Ugh! It made Marigold feel nauseous. She was relieved to have Luke to talk to.

'Did you find your mum's whereabouts on the net?'

'Not a squeak – disappeared into thin air, she has. Good luck to her.' Luke studied his fingernails, as though he hadn't a care in the world, but his face betrayed him.

Marigold wished she could make him feel better, but she didn't know how. What do you do to cheer up a semi-ghost? That wasn't something she'd ever come across in PHSE classes.

More to the point, she was beginning to feel hungry. She opened the fridge to find only wine and champagne, three fat-free yoghurts and a solitary half lemon. Not much to sustain a healthy girl there, she thought.

'Dad,' she ventured, when at last he came up for air, 'what time is our table booked for?'

Her father disentangled his left arm from its Bunny-clinch and consulted his watch. 'God, is that the time?' he said. 'We'd better get a move on, girls.' Marigold cringed, *girls*, whatever next?

'I must repair my face,' Bunny simpered. 'Won't be a moment.' Then she popped her head back round the door, 'And what about you, Marigold? Do you need to freshen up?'

'No thanks. I'm just fine as I am,' Marigold said, glaring at the retreating figure.

'Watch it,' her father warned.

'Don't worry, I'll be good as gold, I promise.' To keep her mind off the prospect of an evening in the embarrassing company of ancient love-birds, Marigold began to count the polished floorboards. That kept her going until at last Bunny returned, lipsticked, sprayed and smelling of something dark and secret.

'Will I do, Ollie?' she asked, doing a twirl, the deep neckline leaving little to the imagination and lots of thigh flashing from a split skirt.

'You look beautiful, my darling. Doesn't she, Kid?' Although Bunny was chicken-bone thin, Dad was obviously besotted with her. He must have forgotten he liked a woman with a decent bit of meat on her – and, come to think of it, he himself looked as though he'd lost weight. Had he been consciously dieting over the last month or so? She tried to remember when she'd last seen him eat a proper meal.

On the way out to the car, Bunny made a grab for Dad's arm, making it plain he was her property now. Marigold reluctantly followed in their wake, wishing she was somewhere – anywhere – else. Luke shadowed her every step. He didn't trust this Bunny-woman an inch and tried to lighten the proceedings by making exaggerated kiss-kiss noises on the back of his hand – anything to make Marigold smile.

'Ssh!' She felt laughter welling in her throat. It was difficult enough trying to keep a straight face watching Dad and the dreadful Bunny acting like teenagers without Luke making silly noises, but as no-one else could see him, perhaps he couldn't be heard either.

The evening turned out to be even worse than she'd imagined. Dad ushered his *girls* into the restaurant, all flustered apologies for turning up late. Marigold was stunned, the place was incredibly stylish - bucket seats built into the wall, trendy pottery on the window sills, low-lit. Not Dad's usual style, he was more a Pizza Express man. Not now, obviously.

Almost beyond hunger by this time, Marigold tried to remember what she'd had to eat that day - a bar of chocolate, half a biscuit and some crisps hardly counted as a meal. She studied the menu as closely as an exam text. At least it gave her something to do with her hands and a focus for her eyes. Talk about playing gooseberry! Here was her father, her *father,* acting like a man bewitched - she couldn't bear to watch. She had been odd-girl-out with Jocelyn and her various boyfriends from time to time, but she'd never imagined herself in that particular role with her dad and a lady-friend. It took some getting used to.

As soon as the waiter arrived with her meal, Marigold's appetite returned. In short order, she polished off a crab starter followed by peppered steak and chips. When the waitress presented the dessert menu Bunny, who had eaten no more than a green salad, declined prettily. 'What about you, Kid?' Dad asked.

Marigold poured over the range of sweets on offer, trying to decide between Death by Chocolate and apple pie with clotted cream.

'Do you really think you should, my dear?' Bunny's stage whisper could have been heard two tables away. She looked pointedly at the girl's gaping shirt. 'Aren't you just a touch on the plump side for puddings?'

Marigold ignored her. Looking her father straight in the eye, she said, 'Death by Chocolate, please Dad.'

'It's a mistake to encourage her, if you ask me, Ollie.' Bunny dabbed her lips with a napkin. No-one did ask you, thank you very much, Marigold thought, eyeing her with venom. 'She's at a very impressionable stage, Ollie, you shouldn't . . .' She was interrupted by a waterfall of cold white wine cascading down her neckline and into her silken lap. It was as though her hand had been nudged by an invisible force. She jumped up with a squeal, her spiel forgotten. 'Ollie, look what you've made me do! I'm drenched!'

Dad leapt to his feet like he'd trodden on a nail and tried to blot the wine with a napkin as it dripped from Bunny's skirt into her high-heeled sandals. Hard to imagine a wine glass holding that amount of liquid! Marigold felt almost sorry for her dad, knowing he was being unfairly blamed, so she scowled in what she took to be Luke's general direction. Meantime, Bunny kept up her complaint at full volume, 'Look at my dress! My sandals! Ollie, do something!' until finally, a posse of waiters descended on them with soothing words and fresh linen tablecloths.

'Come on, darling. I'll buy you a new dress, if need be. Don't spoil things. It's a special night out for all of us, isn't it?' Dad looked from one to the other, a rabbit caught in the headlights. He reached across the banquette-seat, attempting to bring the two of them into the circle of his arms. In agreement for once, Marigold and Bunny both shrugged him off.

With the mess cleared away and her glass topped up, Bunny went back into attack-mode. She eyed Marigold's calorie-laden dessert with a shudder, 'Well, I don't suppose *one* pudding will make a lot of difference at this stage in the game,' she said. Then, swinging her blonde mane for maximum effect, she decided to forget about Marigold's weight problem and concentrate on charming Oliver. 'Just a small espresso for me, sweetheart,' she said, smiling up at him. 'Someone's got to think of her waistline.'

Dad hadn't dared order a pudding for himself – and apple pie was his absolute favourite. Under the stare of two pairs of eyes, Marigold tucked into her dessert, finishing off every last gungy crumb, every drop of gloopy sauce.

'Thank you, Dad,' she said. 'That was delicious.' Then she excused herself from the table, made a mad dash and silently threw up in the safety of the ladies. She'd had enough. It was a nightmare. Tear-sodden, she sat on the toilet seat in a state of utter despair. The phrase 'a touch on the plump side' really got to her. Bad enough being bullied in the classroom on weekdays, now it was happening on a Saturday evening in a very public place. How could Dad do this to her?

'Buck up, Goldielocks.' The boy had materialised behind the locked door. He pulled off some toilet tissue and gently mopped her face. 'Don't let her see she's got to you.' He was right, of course. Gradually her coughing and spluttering came to a stop. She unlocked the door, washed her face in cold water and ran a comb through her hair. It bounced back, red-gold curls bobbing on her shoulders.

'That's the ticket!' Luke sounded more like a jolly grandfather than an almost-dead 15-year-old. Maybe ghosts were programmed to talk like that. 'What did you think of my wine-spilling effort?'

'Brilliant – except that Dad got the blame.'

'You can't have everything in this life.' Luke sounded pretty pleased with his party trick.

The thought of Bunny sitting there in wet clothes quite cheered Marigold up. She managed a smile of sorts, put her head in the air and marched out to the car park. Not long now, she thought. But she was wrong. She had to endure another couple of excruciating hours in Bunny's apartment before Dad took notice of her exaggerated yawns and they set off for home.

'Enjoy yourself tonight, Kiddo?'

'A bit, but not in a good way.' Still, the evening was over and done with. Nothing could be worse than the night Mum had left, she reminded herself. If she could survive that, she could survive anything.

Marigold wondered where Luke had gone this time – there was no sign of him in the car. Nor in the house. Pity. Just as she was getting used to his presence around the place. Maybe he'd done his good deed for the day. Maybe his looking-after stint was over. But he might have had the decency to say good-bye first.

For once, she was looking forward to school on Monday. She'd have a ball unpicking the Dad-and-Bunny saga with Jocelyn who loved gossip. She'd be fascinated and shocked in equal measures.

As she fell asleep, Marigold wondered if Luke would manage to stick around long enough to be paraded in front of the girls at the end-of-term disco, or even better, the T-in-the-Park gig the Heligan Gardens had been promised. Now, that would be a feather in her cap. I'll ask him next time he materalises, she thought, imagining being partnered by such a tall handsome guy – even the strange blue eyes gave him a certain something. The trouble was, Luke couldn't be summoned at will, he worked to a timetable all of his own. So tonight, just when she'd have liked a word with him, not a sign, not a sound. It was obviously one of his off-duty nights.

CHAPTER FOUR

ON SUNDAY NIGHT, however, the dream-thing came back with a vengeance. No friendly Luke this time, only the Boy, stony-eyed as ever, not the kind of bloke you'd want to accompany you to a disco. Just as well she hadn't got around to inviting him. They seemed to be alone in a windowless cellar. To a claustrophobic, it was scary in the extreme. He made no move and simply gazed at her in complete silence for several minutes. Rattled by his sinister appearance, she looked round frantically for something to count. Nothing. So she sat on the cold stone floor and fell back on the old fingers-and-toes routine that used to help when she was little. Fingers first, then toes. Back to fingers, over and over.

The boy spoke at last, 'Five on each hand, five on each foot, I think you'll find.'

'I thought you'd given up this dream lark? Haven't you got better things to do?'

'Like what?'

'Finding your mum, learning to fly –'

'No wings, remember?'

'Coming to terms with being dead. . .'

'I told you, I'm only halfway there.' His eyes grew bluer than ever, almost as though they had been lit up from behind. There was little left of the jolly young man who'd been around over the weekend.

Marigold shivered. 'Well, I wish you'd hurry up and get out of my life.'

'Can't. Not until you're sorted out – and the way things are going, you're going to need me one day soon.'

'How do you mean?'

'I don't know exactly.' He thought for a moment. 'I have to wait for orders from on-high – they don't take kindly to you doing your own thing.'

'Sounds like Dotheboys Hall!'

'The thing is, they're just voices and you never get to see them.' In his mind's eye, he conjured up the disembodied voices and shivered. By comparison his old headmaster and the house-father seemed almost jolly, at least they had faces, pretty ugly mugs both of them, but recognisable features just the same. 'Someone's out to get you, girl, I'm pretty sure of that.' He gathered his strength and pushed hard against the wall. It fell away, like a bubble bursting. 'Come on,' he said.

Marigold felt a sudden rush of fresh air. She took huge gulps of it. Now they were moving in tandem across a field, not exactly walking, not exactly floating, but something in between, long grass swishing at their legs. The boy stopped and for a fleeting moment, took both her hands in his. He was surprisingly gentle. 'Take care, Goldielocks. I mean it.' And he was gone.

'Luke,' she called. 'Luke!' No reply. She ran, tripped like you do in dreams, and was catapulted body first, stomach after, into a dense forest. Thoroughly frightened, she began to count the trees surrounding her, '. . . twenty-two, twenty-three, twenty-four . . .' She woke to find herself counting aloud. Luke was perched on the end of her bed.

'Where was I?' she asked, a break in her voice.

'In a dream, Sunshine. Don't worry,' Luke, the matey day-time Luke, soothed.

'That's not what I mean,' she said, distraught. 'I've lost count. I'll have to start again.' But the trees had vanished, along with the dream. Trying not to panic, she looked round the familiar room and started on the books arranged in alphabetical order on the bookshelves above her bed. 'One, two, three, four . . .'

'You'll miss the school bus if you don't hurry up,' Luke said.

Like an echo, Dad called up the stair, 'Marigold, you'll miss the bus if you don't get a move on.'

'Didn't I tell you?' Luke smirked, disappearing as Dad's head came round the bedroom door.

'Coming,' Marigold promised, although she'd only got as far as R for Rowling, JK. Now that she'd started, she wouldn't be satisfied until she got to Zephaniah, Benjamin. Pulling on grey trousers and school sweatshirt, eyes racing along the spines, she counted for dear life. As she grabbed for her trainers, she gasped, '125,' and immediately felt a calm, like a passing shower, wash over her. She pulled a brush through her hair and ran downstairs.

'No thanks, Dad, no time for breakfast this morning,' she called over her shoulder as she made for the bus stop.

'How did it go?' Jocelyn wanted to know.

'Don't ask.'

'Not so good? Well, my weekend was no picnic either.' She started on a graphic account of life with her twin cousins, assorted dreary uncles and aunts and her horribly strict grandmother. There was a pause. 'You haven't been listening to a word I've said,' she accused.

Marigold looked at her friend's crestfallen face. 'I'm sorry.'

'Not to worry, come on, spit it out! You've something humungous on your mind, I can tell.'

They edged closer to one another, blanking out the Monday-morning noise of the other kids. 'Can you keep a secret, Joss?'

'What do you take me for? Course I can. Shoot!'

'Well it turns out that my dad's got a girlfriend. . .'

'So? Your mum's out of the picture, after all.'

'But it seems to be deadly serious. They were all over one another on Saturday night, cuddling, snogging – everything. Yuk! I tell you it's been 'Bunny-this' and 'Bunny-that' ever since.'

'Bunny? You're kidding.'

'Cross my heart. . .' and the two looked at one another, descending into a fit of helpless giggles.

'Bunny,' they snorted. *'Bunny!'*

Once they were able to breathe again, Jocelyn asked, 'What's she like?'

'Skinny, long blonde hair, lovely clothes, in fact, everything about her is perfect.'

'But?'

The bus pulled up outside the school gates and the girls stumbled off into a jostling crowd of teenagers, draped with swinging book-bags and sports kit. It wasn't until break they had the opportunity to take up Marigold's story where she had left off.

'Kit-Kat?' Jocelyn offered, breaking her biscuit in two.

'No thanks.'

'You off your food?'

Marigold ignored the question. 'Turns out that she, Bunny that is, teaches fashion at the college. She's intent on taking me on a shopping spree,' she said.

'Lucky old you!'

'I know you'd love the idea to bits, but I can't think of anything worse. Imagine spending a hot Saturday afternoon mooching around the shops trying on tops and trousers – or worse skirts and dresses. Can you see me in a *frock?'*

'I don't know what you're complaining about. Sounds good to me!'

'It's OK for you, you're a size 10. I can never find anything to fit, 18s are disgusting, all old-lady stuff, not that you'd know about that – and anyway, my dad can't afford it. He's always going on about money – or lack of it.'

With that, a couple of the Y8s loomed up behind Jocelyn and made her jump. 'Did Fatso tell you she's got a boyfriend? Thinks he's no end of a tough guy!'

Curiosity, and a touch of respect, lit Jocelyn's eyes. As the bell went, she whispered, 'Is it true?'

'No, yes . . . sort of. Tell you later,' Marigold said as they parted, she to the library, Jocelyn to the science lab. How to get out of this? she wondered. She could hardly tell her best friend that she kept meeting a boy from out of her dreams. Joss'd have her locked up – worse, the gossip would spread like wildfire and she'd be a laughing stock.

And yet, she couldn't help feeling a smidgin of pride about it all. Acquiring a boyfriend had put her up a few notches in Jocelyn's estimation. If only Luke could come out as a real-live person, she'd be up sides with the other girls. After all, he's totally fit, tall, fair hair, blue eyes – what more could a girl ask?

It wasn't only Marigold's wardrobe that Bunny had in her sights, little by little, it was their whole way of life.

Since the original meeting hadn't caused any serious sparks to fly, Dad felt it safe to invite Bunny back to their place. Father and daughter spent time sprucing it up, cleaning and polishing within an inch of its life. Everything that wasn't nailed down was tidied out of sight and Dad even defrosted the fridge.

'Mum would never believe it,' Marigold said.

'Well, she's not likely to get a chance. Not now.'

'Now that she's not here or now that you've met Bunny?'

'Both,' he said, absently burnishing an already shining table-top. 'I never expected to feel this way again – not after your mum – I mean, it's always been just your mum and me, and you, of course . . .' He stopped, returned the polish to its cupboard under the sink, and looked round the kitchen, appraising it like an estate agent. 'It'll have to do. I hope she'll like it.'

Marigold found a clean towel and hung it in the bathroom. When she came back, she said, 'Dad, is it serious? Between you and Bunny, I mean?'

'I'm not sure, but I think it might be.' He grabbed a tea-towel, gave a last flourish to the worktop and looked up. 'It'll be OK with you, love, won't it?'

Like hell it will, she thought, but Dad looked so anxious that she couldn't bear to disappoint him. 'S'pect so. I'll do my best, I promise.' She was rewarded with one of his old-time bear-hugs. 'That's my girl,' he said.

It proved to be the hardest promise she had ever made.

RIVER POLICE CALLED IN read an inside-page headline in *The Guardian*, a week or two out of date. Marigold found it wrapped around a cabbage she'd bought in the market. As ever, she couldn't resist the printed word.

'So help me,' the rescued driver told one of our reporters, 'I had a boy in the van with me, a lad of about 15 or so, maybe 16, not sure. Picked him up off the M5 junction outside Exeter. Funny lad he was, said he was going to Cornwall to look after his granny's dog. Didn't say much else. Couldn't get a word out of him, in fact.'

The van had been lifted out in pretty poor condition and the driver breathalysed before being carted off to hospital, but there was no sign of a boy's body despite the best efforts of several divers. According to the report, the police had been called in once again and the river dredged as far as the estuary. *'If the body of this anonymous young man eventually turns up, it may well be on the foreshore many miles away,' a police spokeswoman told our reporter. She added, 'The case has not been closed.'*

Luke, thought Marigold, tearing the article out and zipping it into her back pocket, it can only be him. He'll want to read about the lost body (his lost body) when, or if, he returns. She hadn't seen him for days, either in real life or in her dreams. Perhaps it's because he's properly dead and doesn't need to keep coming back. Perhaps he's been sent off to guard some other poor soul. She turned over various scenarios in her mind, each one more fanciful than the last. It bugged her that she couldn't get hold of him, text him or whatever, that she had to wait until it suited him to turn up – if ever. The trouble was, she didn't understand much about this dying business – as far as she knew, if you were dead, you stayed that way. But Luke's death was different, that much was obvious.

'Come clean, what about this boyfriend then?' Jocelyn had asked.

'Oh, nothing to it really, just a boy we used to know way back. He was on a visit to . . . our next door neighbours,' she improvised.

'And?'

'And he walked me along to the library – that's all.'

'Has he got a name, this mysterious boy?'

'Luke,' Marigold said, bounced into the truth.

'How did your Luke make such an impression on the Y8s?'

'He's not *my* Luke – but you should have seen the punch he landed!' She smiled at the memory of Kevin Jenkins lying flat on his back in the grass.

'I wish I'd been a fly on the wall – or a bird in the tree,' Jocelyn said. 'Message me next time your hero comes back this way.'

'Nice to hear that someone wants to know me,' said a familiar voice, although there was no sign of Luke himself.

'Shut up,' a fierce whisper.

'What?' Jocelyn asked.

'Nothing.'

'There's something odd about you these days. I can't quite put my finger on it. Maybe you're in love – that's it, you're in love, Mari.'

Despite herself, Marigold felt a blush rise to her cheeks. 'Don't be ridiculous,' she said, looking at her watch. 'Anyway, I've got to go. State visit from Bunny tonight.'

By this time, Bunny had really begun to make her mark. It had started with Dad whose clothes had been smartened up considerably. No more T-shirts and jeans, now he was into smart casual in a big way.

Gradually, as she had become an all-too frequent visitor, the house also came under Bunny's scrutiny, small changes at first – a set of matching mugs, flowers tastefully arranged in a vase, a spanking new tea-towel, finally a pair of fur-edged pink rubber gloves appeared by the kitchen sink. How yuk can you get? Marigold wondered, as she tried to find a hiding place for the repulsive things.

A toothbrush in the bathroom will be next, she thought. And she was right. In no time at all, the toothbrush arrived, an electric one at that – accompanied by a bulging make-up bag, skin freshener, shower gel, a set of miniature nail varnish bottles in rainbow colours and hundreds of mysterious creams and perfumes unfamiliar to Marigold who managed very well with shampoo and the occasional jar of Christmas bath salts. Her mother had never been interested in this kind of thing either, simply following her own mother's soap and water strictures.

Bunny's Marigold-make-over campaign started in earnest one Friday evening. As soon as she stepped from her car, long-legged and elegant as a gazelle, she treated Dad to a perfunctory kiss, saying, 'No time for all that now, Ollie, you'll smudge my make-up,' as she shoved him away. Taking the rebuff in his stride, he was surprised to be dispatched to the supermarket to replenish the wine, but did as he was told. This meant Marigold would be left alone with Superwoman. She shrank inside herself. I'd better get used to it, she thought, remembering her promise. However, as she was drawn into the now-familiar air-kissing procedure, she realised that this girls-together session had been expertly engineered. Bunny consulted her diary.

'I could do the 17th,' she said, in a breathy whisper, 'just you and me off for a bit of retail therapy. How does that appeal?'

'Doesn't. I hate shopping and I've got all the clothes I need,' Marigold muttered, adding, 'Thank you, all the same,' for politeness sake.

'Nonsense,' Bunny said, 'it's a girly thing. You'll love it, I promise. And look at you . . .' She stood back, Trinny-style, narrowed her eyes and took stock. 'I do believe you've lost a pound or two, but in all honesty, you could do with a bit of help.'

Rude cow, Marigold thought, attempting to stare her out, although it didn't work. Bunny simply smiled a particularly cheesy smile, saying, 'Don't worry, dear . . .' *(Dear!* A teeth-clenching word if ever there was one!) '. . . we'll soon get you sorted out. I expect we can find something . . . floaty perhaps, loose . . . yes, something to minimise that puppy-fat.' Then quickly, confidently, tapping the girl on her midriff, 'You mustn't mind me – I'm a very direct person, you'll find.'

You can say that again. Marigold was determined not to let Dad down, so she folded her lips and bit back the words. Silently furious, she turned her attention to the table, banging the cutlery down with quite unnecessary force. Under her breath, she counted out three knives, three forks, then one, two, three place mats, glasses, paper napkins. This time round, counting didn't work its usual magic. She dug her nails into her wrist – hard. Puppy-fat, *puppy-fat,* I'll show you, lady, she thought.

She flounced off upstairs to her bedroom, leaving Bunny to flit between cooker and table. It wasn't as though she actually *cooked,* but she was a dab-hand at opening expensive supermarket ready meals. Anything to impress her father.

When Dad got back, he and Bunny settled on the couch to enjoy a kissing session and few pre-dinner glasses of wine. When the bottle was empty, Dad summoned Marigold to the table. Decorated with a centre-piece of flower-heads and tall candles, it looked unfamiliar, like a rich relation of itself. Marigold had to agree that the meal was delicious, from the asparagus starter, through minted lamb to the raspberry Pavlova with lashings of cream. She ate every scrap, even having seconds of pudding.

As soon as possible, she excused herself, locked the bathroom door, stuck her finger down her throat and made herself sick. It was a disgusting thing to do, but she was getting quite good at it – and it was beginning to work. She was sure she'd lost the best part of a stone. Puppy-fat! She'd show them! A squirt of air-freshener and a quick session of tooth-brushing and she was ready for any barb Bunny could throw at her.

What she hadn't counted on was Luke, who was waiting in the shadows at the top of the stairs. 'Idiot,' he said. 'You'll make yourself ill if you go on like this.'

'Who cares?'

'I do, for one.' Perhaps he really does fancy me, Marigold thought. Pity he's not flesh and bone, just my luck to be stuck with a half-dead boyfriend. 'And I expect your mum does too,' he added quietly.

'Mum? She's lost interest in me that's for sure. I haven't seen or heard of her for months.' Marigold carried the thought that her mother didn't want her like a heavy lump inside her chest. She kept it secret, hidden from view, didn't talk about it much.

'Give it a try – you might be surprised.'

'What makes you a world expert on mothers all of a sudden? You don't even know if yours is alive or dead, do you? Seen this?' She dug out the scrap of old newspaper. Luke frowned over the story.

'They won't find me, you know – at least, not yet.'

'D'you mean, you're going to be hanging around me forever?'

'One day you'll appreciate me, honestly you will.'

'Can't wait . . .' But for the moment, Marigold had had enough of everyone – of Luke, of Bunny, even of Dad who had changed, and not for the better. To keep the peace, she knew she'd have to psych herself up for the promised shopping trip one day soon. She slammed the bedroom door in Luke's face. 'And don't you try to follow me!' she hissed.

'I wouldn't dream of it . . .' a faint voice from the landing.

And he kept to his word. For the best part of a week, Marigold saw nothing of him, either in dreamtime or daytime. Soon she stopped expecting to hear his voice or see him appear round the corner. Perhaps they've found his body, she thought, although she had heard nothing about it on the news. Maybe he's found peace at last. But it niggled that he hadn't made time to say good-bye.

'Aren't you going to introduce me to the boyfriend, then?' Jocelyn sounded quite miffed.

'I told you, he's gone.'

'Where?'

'Not sure.'

'Come off it, you must know where he lives – mobile number, email address?'

'Well, I don't.' As well she might, Jocelyn looked sceptical.

'Suit yourself.' And she wandered off, hoping for juicer gossip elsewhere.

True to her word, on the 17th, Bunny picked Marigold up at what she called 'the crack of dawn', although it was nearer ten o'clock. They made for the A39 into Truro and the girly trip was on. Once out of the car park, all excitement and clattering bracelets, Bunny swept everything before her. Marigold trailed in her wake, bored before they were properly started. The Top Shops and New Looks were spurned in favour of fancy boutiques, hidden away up narrow alleyways. Bunny was in her element as she rattled along miles of hangers, selecting great armfuls of clothes in garish colours. She thrust them into Marigold's hands. 'Got to get you out of all that dreary stuff,' she said, snatching yet another pair of cut-offs, emerald green this time.

'I can't wear these,' Marigold protested.

'Why on earth not?'

'I don't do bright . . .'

'We'll see,' Bunny said. 'Just try them on. Give your dad a nice surprise.'

Gritting her teeth, Marigold wriggled into the green trousers and was pleased to find that they zipped up without the usual amount of trouble.

'Try this top.' An arm appeared round the curtain with a jade and black zigzag-striped number, followed by a short waistcoat thing in charcoal that skimmed her (much reduced) spare tyre. 'That's better, takes the tubby look away.' *Tubby look!* Bunny made Marigold sound like a Toby jug. The woman had an eye for fashion, she had to admit, but it most definitely wasn't for her.

'No, Bunny,' she said. 'I can't. It's not me.' Bunny sighed, but she wasn't defeated. Marigold was bullied into tees, halter-necks, bootleg jeans and a couple of swirly skirts. She had never had so many new clothes all at once in her entire life. Eventually, she and Bunny fell into a café, ordered Americanos and sat surrounded by bags and carriers from expensive boutiques Marigold had never known existed.

However, not everything was destined exclusively for Marigold's wardrobe. Bunny had done rather well for herself too. She peered inside a shiny drawstring bag, 'What do you think of these?' she asked, carefully undoing black tissue paper to reveal drop earrings in turquoise and silver.

'Very nice,' Marigold said without much enthusiasm. The woman must have dozens of the things, a different pair for every day of the year. She had cats and tigers, birds of paradise and Christmas trees, not to mention a collection of gold hoops and hand-crafted silver spirals. Marigold would have been amused to discover that Bunny's students laid bets on the next set of earrings to take her fancy.

'We'll need to soften your dad's edges a bit before he sees what we've been up to this afternoon. A really good bottle of wine should do the trick!' Bunny had gone all giggly and girly. 'I don't expect he thought we'd give the card such a beating - but it's all in a good cause. We'll wow him between us!'

'This didn't all come off Dad's card, did it?' Marigold was appalled. She knew how strapped her father was for cash these days. As far as she knew, he still put money into Mum's account every month, 'I'm no skinflint,' he had said. 'Just because your mum isn't under my roof at the moment, it doesn't mean I can forget about her.' Then there were all the new bits and pieces for the house that Bunny thought essential, Dad's updated gear and meals out in various expensive restaurants. Marigold felt quite sick

– nothing to do with bingeing this time, more the thought of the amount of money they'd spent in one morning.

'I don't need any of this stuff,' she said. 'We can take it back if the labels are still on, can't we?'

'Money's not a problem, as it happens.' Bunny was full of confidence. 'We're sharing expenses now, your dad and I,' she said, reapplying her lip-gloss and gazing with apparent satisfaction into her handbag mirror. News to me, Marigold thought.

'Well, let's go and face the music.' They retrieved Bunny's car and set off home. Marigold tried to add up what they'd spent, but her mental arithmetic wasn't up to it. It was a lot, much too much. She was too worried to utter a word.

'Anything wrong?' Bunny enquired. Marigold made a non-committal sound, just managing to keep this side of her promise to Dad.

However, her father appeared delighted when they displayed their purchases. 'Give us a twirl, Kid,' he said, when Marigold was persuaded to show off a red halter-neck top and a long slim skirt with an up-to-the-minute handkerchief hem. 'I didn't imagine I'd ever see my daughter looking quite so glamorous. Congratulations, my darling!' He kissed the nape of Bunny's neck.

She looked over her shoulder at Marigold. 'Didn't I tell you he'd be over the moon?'

Exhausted, Marigold mooched upstairs to get into something more comfortable – and more her style. She was taken aback to hear a wolf-whistle echoing along the hall. Luke.

'Suits you,' he said.

'Back again, like a bad penny?' she greeted him. 'I thought perhaps you were a goner now they've found your body, but no such luck, obviously.'

The following weekend started out bright and sunny, gearing up to be yet another day of searing heat. *'meet u at the shed, mst get out of hr pronto.'*

'ok,' Jocelyn had texted back, eager for a gossip session. 'Rabbit trouble?' she asked, as the two girls chose a seat in the shade of a stripy umbrella – a Continental touch in the middle of Falmouth.

'Too true, she stays overnight several times a week now. Today was scheduled for yet another shopping trip – she tries to organise every minute of my life, Dad's too, now that the college is on holiday – and he goes along with it, a silly smile on his face.'

'That's love for you.' Jocelyn imitated violin music, looking so lugubrious that Marigold had to laugh. 'A latte?' she suggested. 'And a doughnut?'

'Latte, yes. Doughnut, no.' Jocelyn ordered the coffee and two doughnuts. 'Go on,' she said. 'My treat.'

Marigold's mouth was watering. 'Can't, unfortunately. I'm on a diet.'

Jocelyn eyed her friend critically. 'Mmm,' she said, 'you do seem to have lost a bit of weight. That Bunny's doing too? Or is it love?'

'What is it with you these days? No, I am not, repeat not, in love. If I do manage to lose weight, it's nothing to do with . . .' She bit off the name.

'Luke?'

Marigold glared. 'It's just to spite her, Bunny. She thinks I'm gross . . .'

'Did she really say that?'

'Not on so many words, but that's what she thinks. She steers me to Big Girl shops, talks about disguising my puppy-fat – did you ever hear such utter crap?'

'Well, you're beginning to look pretty good – the Marigold I used to know wouldn't have worn that red halter top in a hundred years. Suits you.'

'Don't you start! I only put it on to keep the peace.' She gazed at the doughnut Jocelyn was eating, at her tongue capturing the sprinkled sugar. 'OK, you win. I'll have the other one.' She crammed it into her mouth, revelling in the sugar burst. Immediately she hated what she'd done, I *am* gross, she taunted herself. 'S'cuse me,' and she was off to throw up, yet again. Mind you, she thought, as she had to admit that the pounds were coming off. Even Dad had noticed and he didn't notice a lot – unless it was Bunny-shaped.

Once they had finished their coffees, the girls were at a loss. 'What now?' Jocelyn said. The waitress cleared the cups away, aggressively swabbing their table. 'Anything more?' she asked.

Marigold couldn't bear to do the shops again, the beach would be crowded, the cinema out of the question in such heat and she had no intention of going back to the house, to Bunny, to her increasingly unfamiliar Dad. Something Luke said came into her mind.

'Fancy going to St Ives?'

'In this heat – it'll be swarming with tourists!' Jocelyn didn't sound too keen. 'Isn't that where your mum's hanging out?' she asked.

Although Marigold didn't think she was ready for a one-to-one with her mother, she couldn't help being curious. 'Maybe we could just walk past her cottage,' she suggested. 'It's not actually in the town – everyone will be on the beach on a day like this. Go on, Joss. I'd really like to see what it looks like, but I don't want to talk to her – not yet, not until the Bunny thing is above board, and that's Dad's business, not mine.'

They strolled along to the Dell, boarded the train and, at last, Marigold relaxed. 'This is a hundred times better than shopping.'

'Whatever turns you on.' Jocelyn wasn't altogether convinced. Shopping was high on her list of fun things to do, especially if someone was throwing money around. But Marigold had been in a strange mood of late, so she was prepared to give her quirky ideas a go, just this once.

Two trains later, and they found themselves chuntering along the single line from St Erth to St Ives. The carriage was bulging with tourists vying with one another for sea-side seats. It was noisy, exciting and a million miles away from their usual Saturday afternoon haunts. Best of all, from Marigold's point of view, Luke was nowhere to be seen.

The cottage stood at the top of the town, at the end of a rutted lane. 'Get that view!' Marigold stopped, entranced. Far below, cradled in a curve of sea so blue that artists come from around the world to paint it, the town hunkered down under moss-tiled roofs. Sunlight splashed an old-gold light over everything it touched. Mesmerised by the view, Marigold sat on a tourist-friendly bench.

Impatient, Jocelyn pulled on her arm. 'Come on, if we're going.'

'Just trying to come up with a word for the colour of the sea, sapphire? azure? peacock? What d'you think?'

'It's blue, you nerd!'

'You've got no soul, Joss.' But she got to her feet and followed Jocelyn along the lane.

Her mother's garden was a blaze of flowers climbing over one another, all higgledy-piggledy, 'And I bet she doesn't know the names of any of them,' Marigold laughed.

'Does it matter?' Jocelyn was pragmatic about most things. 'It looks fantastic.'

Marigold put on her sunglasses and tried to slink past the fence, keeping a wary eye on the blue front door. 'Do you think she'll recognise me?'

'Of course she will – you're her daughter, after all!'

'Not so's you'd notice.' But she had no need to worry. The curtains were drawn against the sunlight and the door remained firmly closed. There was no sign of life.

'What now?'

They meandered to the end of the lane and flopped down in the shade of trees heavy with summer leaves. It was gloriously peaceful, the only sound, bees fizzing in the long grass, the sea murmuring in the distance. Even the birds were stunned into silence by the heat.

The girls leaned back against a low stone wall, too hot to talk. Jocelyn fanned her face with her hat while Marigold idly picked moss from between the stones. She arranged the tufts in neat rows. Then they saw the cow. Pure white, she minced daintily along the open road, udder swinging. She stopped, gazed intently at the girls from long-lashed eyes and helped herself to the moss, laid out so enticingly on the wall. She belched gently, switched flies off her back and sashayed towards them. Again, she held them in a steady stare. It reminded Marigold of Luke in dream-thing mode.

'That cow knows something we don't, I swear,' she said.

'You'll be hearing voices next.' Jocelyn scoffed. The cow swished her tail, dipped her head and sauntered slowly off, turning now and again to look at the girls.

'Follow the white cow.' Marigold heard the voice she knew well. She looked up. If Luke was around, he had kept himself well hidden.

'Let's see where she goes,' she suggested to Jocelyn. 'She might be lost.'

'Cows don't get lost.' But, curiosity getting the better of them and having nothing more urgent on their minds, the girls followed her, walking carefully to avoid the cowpats. At the river's edge they stopped. A police tape warned them to go no further. A tent had been erected on the river bank and police in boots and plastic gloves stood in huddles.

'Do you think they've found a body?' Jocelyn asked, the cow forgotten.

Marigold shivered, Luke, she thought. And the heat seemed to drain from the afternoon sun.

CHAPTER FIVE

WHEN SHE GOT home, he was waiting for her. He watched her kick off her sandals and throw herself across the bed. She was sticky with sweat and prickly with worry. 'So they've managed to find your body at long last?'

'A false alarm,' he said. 'I thought I'd better let you know.'

'Then, why pull the cow stunt?' She tried to sound cross, cool, not daring to show how pleased she was that he was still around.

'I wanted to sort of warn you and – well, I hoped you'd be able to help. You see, they found my mum . . . in the river.'

'Dead?' she asked in a voice so quiet, she barely recognised it as her own.

'No, not yet – the *Packet* got it right, it seems – she's still around,' he smiled – one of his thin wintry smiles. 'It would take more than a dip in the river to kill *my* mother off. Apparently she floated – full of booze or something, I expect. Anyway, she was doing her Ophelia bit, still clutching a bunch of wild flowers when they rescued her.'

'So why bring us into it?'

'Well, I know that you two go nowhere without your mobiles, so I thought you could have dialled 999 or whatever.'

'Couldn't you have sent a text like any other civilised human being?'

'I'm no longer classed as human, remember? Anyway, ghosts and mobiles don't mix, we mess up the phone mast frequencies something horrible. I simply wanted to attract your attention without Jocelyn cottoning on to my existence – or,' with a cross between a snort and a giggle, 'should I say non-existence?' He gazed out of Marigold's bedroom window, twiddling absently with the blind cord.

'Careful, you'll have that in a knot,' she warned.

'As it turned out, there was no need for you girls, a birder spotted my mother, fished her out and called an ambulance. Then the plods arrived, so I made myself scarce.'

'Taken her to Treliske, have they?'

'I suppose.'

'Aren't you going to find out?'

'Visit the hospital? No way. The sight of my face would bring on a heart attack. I don't want to be responsible for my mother's sudden death on the top of everything else. And another thing, apparently I'm on the wanted list.'

'Wanted? What for?'

'Not seen the posters yet? They're putting mugshots of me all over the place. *Have you seen this person? Any information . . .* blah, blah, blah . . . It's a complete cock-up – I daren't get picked up till you're sorted out.' Marigold glared.

'Perhaps you haven't noticed, but I don't need *sorting out,* especially by you.'

'Forget it, Goldielocks. I'm feeling pretty messed up right now.' For a moment, he seemed lost for words, then quietly, 'My mother looks pretty good, you know, considering how long she's been in the water.'

Marigold couldn't believe how callous he sounded – it was his mum he was talking about, after all. I suppose he has his reasons, she thought, but even so? She didn't know what to say.

'Cat got your tongue?' Luke asked, holding her gaze with those stone-blue eyes. He sounded more flippant than he felt. At this precise moment, he needed human comfort more than anything else and reached out to touch the girl's bare arm, but quickly let the idea drop. You didn't take that kind of liberty with Marigold, he'd cottoned on to that. 'Hope she makes it – drowning's getting to be a habit in our family.'

'Did you get to talk to her?'

'No – in a way I wish I had.'

'What are you waiting for? You're invisible. It shouldn't be a problem to drop by Treliske and see how she's doing.' Luke hesitated. 'Go on,' she said. 'It will give you something to do.'

'You'll be OK without me?'

'Of course I will. I'm one tough cookie, I have to be! I wish you'd get that into your thick head . . .' But she was talking to thin air.

She had to assume that Luke had gone. He certainly was no longer visible. Although he could be an absolute pain in the butt, she couldn't help feeling sorry for him. At least she still had two parents, an absent mother and a lovesick father, to be sure, but undeniably of this world – and she herself was still alive. She pinched herself hard just to make sure.

Her trouble was that the lack of food, real food, was beginning to take its toll. It made her feel dizzy, 'feathery' she called it, as not only her energy, but her concentration, gradually slipped away. She found homework tiresome and, to the dismay of her teachers, her marks plummeted. But she didn't care, she no longer had to search among the 18s – in fact, if she breathed in, she could inch herself into a pair of size 14 jeans. That made it all worthwhile. She had taped a motto to the inside of her wardrobe door, *Nothing tastes as good as skinny feels.* And it would get better, she promised herself, what was all this about size zero? She was convinced she had willpower in spades. She'd show them!

Instead of lamp-posts and trees, clothes pegs and socks, life became one round of counting calories – one small boiled potato 80, one medium apple 60, an orange 44, a mini-tub of cottage cheese 96, she knew them all off by heart, even a single slice of cucumber, which she hated, came in at 10. It became an obsession.

'What's the matter with you, Kid?' her dad grumbled. 'You're all fads and fancies these days, never have time to sit down at the table, always off somewhere in a rush. Boyfriend trouble, is it? Bring him back here so that your old dad can give him the once-over.' He gave her an outrageous wink and went back to mumbling sweet nothings into his mobile, so presumably Bunny was on the other end.

When she could no longer stomach the lettuce-leaf stuff, Marigold binged, wolfing down great platefuls of food, crisps by the bagful, chocolate biscuits by the packet, bringing everything up later in the privacy of the loo. She began to hate the smell of food, hating herself even more sometimes. Bingeing and being sick was a horrible way to go on, but she imagined that it made her slimming campaign less noticeable.

Marigold had reckoned without Luke. After one of her sicking-up sessions, she found him lounging outside the bathroom door. 'You are positively disgusting!' he informed her.

'So? Who's asking your opinion?' She stepped across the hall to face him. Luke pushed her away.

'Don't come too near,' he said. 'Your breath smells like a sewer. And what's more, your hair's gone all funny.'

Marigold's hair was her best feature. Red-gold and shining, it almost made up for the extra pounds she carried on stomach and hips. She tossed it back, feeling positively defensive.

'It just needs a wash,' she said. 'Now take yourself off, preferably to somewhere in the next world, and leave me alone.' She flounced off to look at herself in the bedroom mirror. Luke was right *of course,* her hair was like a doormat, but her waistband was beginning to gape. Great, she thought, all I need now is a glug of mouthwash to deal with the bad breath and some decent conditioner for my hair. She wondered if Bunny would notice if she tried some of hers, but couldn't be bothered to search for it. I don't know why I let that part-time ghost rattle me, she thought, all geared up to have another go at him, but Luke had disappeared – yet again. Only his mocking laughter followed her as she crept downstairs. But this time, he seemed to have gone for good. Her dreams were just dreams, the usual patchwork of the boringly normal school-based, Mum-back-in-her-proper-place stuff.

A couple of weeks later, just as she was getting used to boredom taking over her nights, the dream-thing returned. Every time she closed her eyes, Luke appeared, saying little, just watching her with those stony eyes. Not the quirky day-time Luke she had grown used to, but Luke in the Boy's persona. He stared her out in the old cold way and began to make sleep one long nightmare. She tried everything, stayed up late, left the light on, plugged herself into her iPod, but nothing worked.

She tried to appeal to Luke's better nature. 'What is it? What have I done?'

'Nothing – yet. But they say you're heading for trouble.'

'When you've got it sussed out – if ever – be sure to let me into the secret.' Sarcasm was useless, but it made her feel better. 'Until then, go away and leave me in peace.'

'I can't. I've got to wait.'

'Then wait somewhere else.' Half-awake, Marigold buried her head in her pillow and tried to shut him out. It was no use.

'Try counting sheep,' the boy advised.

'Been there, done that.' But just as the early sun began to light up the sky, she fell into a deep sleep, at last free of the dream-thing.

When she awoke, Luke was waiting perched on the end of her bed, riffling through a book of Brian Patten's love poems. 'Sorry,' he said. 'Sorry about last night.' He smiled in apology. 'I'm going off duty, so you're on your own tonight.'

Marigold struggled to string a few words together. She wasn't often at her best in the morning. 'Suits me,' was the best she could manage. The cistern flushed. She heard Dad on the stairs and reluctantly reached for her towel. If she wanted a shower before Bunny got up, she'd need to get a move on. 'I'd like a bit of privacy,' she told Luke. 'Get going.'

'Don't worry, I'm on my way.'

'Don't let me keep you.' Luke's shape shimmered, as though he was about to dissolve, then he thought better of it.

'Take care,' he said. 'Today could be the day. I tried to warn you last night, but you wouldn't listen.'

'Listen! I didn't get the chance. You were too busy frightening the life out of me.' But she was talking to a blank wall. She made for the bathroom and turned on the shower while the going was good. Quite safe, she reckoned, Bunny would still be enjoying her me-time under the duvet for another half hour, at least.

Breakfast, what was the least she could get away with? A small bowl of Cornflakes, a half-slice of toast, a cup of black coffee? As she went downstairs, Marigold smelled bacon. Dad was grilling bacon, her absolute favourite, how could he?

'I'm doing my Gordon Ramsey this morning,' he grinned. 'Fancy a bacon bap, love?' A fat white bap, crisply-grilled bacon. Temptation on a plate. Marigold couldn't resist it. The bacon roll barely touched the sides. 'Another?'

'Thanks, Dad. Absolutely delicious.' How many calories? Frantically she tried to count, but daren't work out the total. She hated herself for giving in so easily and loathed the ugly fat body she imagined she'd see in the mirror. No wonder they call me names, she thought. She felt the food trapped like a lump in her gullet. The need to sick it up was urgent. But Bunny was firmly ensconced in the bathroom by this time, so she made for the back door.

Any excuse was a good excuse. 'Anything you need from Spar?' she called.

'Where are you off to, girl?' Dad's voice echoed from the kitchen, but she hadn't time to hang around. She had to find a secluded place to throw up – and quick. She sprinted round to the front garden, through the gate and straight across the road. She didn't see Kevin Jenkins leap for his mountain bike and take off at a rate of knots straight into her path.

'You blind or something?' he yelled as he screeched to an abrupt stop, both feet to the floor. Then slowly he began to wheel around in ever decreasing circles. But she wasn't the target this time round. 'Where's the boyfriend then? I'd like a word with him.' He pulled a torn A4 from his pocket and waved it in front of Marigold's face. 'Seen this?'

Marigold made out the word MISSING in bold capitals over a blurry photograph of Luke looking about ten years old. 'It's him, the boyfriend, isn't it? Isn't it?' Kevin was so close, she could feel his saliva as he spat out his questions. 'I bet there's a hefty reward, so let's be having him!' Intimidated by his nearness, she stood rooted to the spot, bereft of words for once. 'Come on, come on! Tell me where I can find him or you'll be sorry!' He let go of the bike and grabbed a handful of Marigold's hair. She screamed.

'Shut up! Shut up, you silly cow!' Kevin put his hand over her mouth, so she bit it. Hard. Surprised, he shoved her into the hedge with his good hand. 'Silly bitch!'

He looked down at his quarry. 'Ready to spill the beans yet?'

'I don't know where he is – honestly I don't.'

'Liar!' But Kevin wasn't finished with her, not yet. He whipped out his mobile and photographed her sprawling in the ditch. 'Fatty Batty Merrick sat on a wall, Fatty Batty Merrick had a big fall!' he sang, snorting with laughter, obviously delighted at his own brand of wit. 'It'll be a winner on Facebook, believe me!'

He reckoned without Marigold's guardian angel. Luke materialised out of nowhere to stand foursquare in the middle of the road. 'This guy giving you grief?' he asked. Marigold felt too ill and out of breath to answer.

Kevin was full of bluster. 'You again?' Stopped in his tracks, he stared hard into Luke's face. 'Ain't the cops looking for you?' He brandished his mobile. 'This'll prove it – might even make the telly tonight.'

'Be sure to take my best side.' Luke grinned widely for the camera.

Kevin snapped and snapped again. 'Bloody thing's not working!' He shook the mobile like a demented percussionist, all the while cursing it roundly. Luke hadn't heard anything quite like it – not even in the kids' home where the language could be pretty ripe.

'Cut it out,' he said quietly. 'Ladies present.'

Kevin had had enough. 'Fatty's no lady,' he muttered. He stuffed the phone into his back pocket and grabbed the abandoned bike. Direct action was called for. He aimed a wheelie at the middle of Luke's chest, but Luke didn't move. Cyclist and bike simply bounced off his body – or perhaps they went right through and out the other side, it was difficult to be sure. He straddled the front wheel, fixing Kevin with a cold hard stare.

'Watch it, mate! You could have killed the girl!'

'Shut your mouth, man!' He tried to wrestle free, but Luke held the bike with surprising strength. Kevin was going nowhere.

Marigold found her voice. She picked herself up, gingerly testing arms and legs. She felt dizzy, but not too bad considering she'd almost been run over. 'When you two have finished shouting at one another, I'd appreciate a bit of peace and quiet.'

Kevin stood up on the pedals. 'Only too glad to oblige,' he said. 'I'll have the cops on to you two. Remember, when they're dishing out rewards, I'm first in the queue.' And with that dark threat, he sped away, with as much bravado as he could manage.

It's hard to vomit in any ladylike way, so Marigold was mortified to find Luke standing over her, watching with delicate distaste. 'Eat something that disagreed with you, Goldielocks?'

Marigold wiped her mouth with a tissue. 'Dad made me a bacon bap,' she explained.

'So what's wrong with that? I could see off a bacon bap right this minute.' Marigold felt distinctly dizzy, so she allowed Luke to help her into the garden.

'What kept you?' she asked. 'Some lifeguard you are!' Luke steered her up the steps. 'What the blazes . . . ?' Beside a scrawled Michelin Man in bright red, the legend, *FATTY BATTY LIV* was sprayed on the door.

'Kevin!' Marigold whispered, appalled. 'So that's what he was up to.' Fatty Batty reverberated in her brain. My own fault, she thought, succumbing to Dad's bacon sandwiches – how could I? All she wanted to do was crawl away to a dark place, see nobody, talk to nobody.

'You obviously interrupted him mid-message,' Luke said. 'You OK?'

'I'm fine. Anyway, it's you he's after, not me.'

'He can't touch me. Don't worry.'

'I won't.' She rushed past him and made for the stairs, but Dad blocked her way, tea-towel slung over his shoulder.

'That didn't take you long,' he observed.

'I didn't get to Spar, Dad. I don't feel too good. OK if I go back to bed for a couple of hours?'

'Come to think,' he said, looking at his daughter closely for the first time. 'You do look a touch under the weather.'

Bunny was busying herself with make-up at her father's bedroom mirror. 'Morning,' she called breezily.

'Morning,' Marigold replied, bolting the bathroom door.

She felt utterly defeated. She'd never had to go to bed in the middle of the morning before – usually she was an up-and-at-'em kind of person. After she'd thrown up, yet again, she felt shivery and only too glad to climb under the duvet. Dad's face appeared round the bedroom door. He looked hassled.

'You OK, girl?'

'I'm fine, Dad. Just leave me alone.' She turned to face the wall, feeling at odds with everything and everybody. 'I wish you'd knock before you come barging in.'

'I don't know what's got into you these days, but I don't like it one little bit,' her father grumbled, hovering in the doorway.

'Ollie!' Bunny's commanding voice echoed up the stairs.

'Marigold's not too well – I don't like to leave her on her own.'

'For goodness sake, she's a big girl, just having a bit of a tantrum, if you ask me.'

Nobody's asking you, Marigold thought, but she said, 'On you go, Dad. Honestly, I'm OK – a bit of a headache, that's all.'

'Ready, Ollie?' Bunny was losing patience.

'Coming.' Marigold heard Dad's feet on the stairs. 'Bye!' he called up as the front door banged. Then the car churning up the gravel and she was on her own at last. Miracle of miracles, neither had noticed the scarlet Michelin Man. If she could raise the energy, she'd have a go at cleaning it off later, she promised herself.

The sun was so bright that she buried her head beneath the pillow and tried not to think – about the dream-thing, about food, about being bullied, about anything. But it wasn't easy. Then the tears started to flow. She felt almost as low as she'd been right after Mum left – even the size 14 jeans hanging in the wardrobe didn't give her a lift today.

To concentrate her mind, she began to count the stars above the bed, Mum's crazy 'diamonds in the sky', but managed no more than 72 before her mobile rang. It made her lose count and she had to start again. Nothing was working out today. She let it go on to 'Missed call', not once, but twice.

Her brain in over-drive, her throat raw, sleep was impossible. Dad, who had depended on her, hand, foot and finger since Mum's departure, no longer needed her now that Bunny was the big thing in his life. It was a wonder she hadn't turned pea-green with jealousy. She was a waste of space, if truth be told. If only she had the bottle, she'd seriously think about doing away with herself. Lucky old Luke, she thought, he's gone and done it.

Luke himself felt far from lucky. He'd been summoned Upstairs, no excuses, the Voice was adamant. Now that was scary. After all, he was still very junior and just learning the ropes.

'You haven't got the hang of this yet, have you, Boy?' Luke was well-used to listening to a commanding voice in his head, but this was different. This was a Super-voice, incredibly sarcastic into the bargain.

'I'm sorry, sir.'

'I'll tell you once more and once only – either go into dream-mode and stay there or get back into your body, but don't keep jumping from one to the other. It is *not* done, got it?'

'Yes, sir. Sorry, sir.'

'And all this faffing about with a white cow – what were you thinking about? We don't do magic – it's serious business up here. Haven't you read the rules? You'll never be eligible for a passport if you don't pull your socks up – and quick about it! Now get going, Boy. Sort that girl out before you contact me again and we'll see where we go from there.'

'Yes, sir. Sorry, sir.'

'You're not going to go through all that sorry-stuff again, I hope.' The Voice dismissed him abruptly.

It was even worse than being made to stand outside the Head's office, Luke thought – and he'd had lots of practice at that. He'd have to go through the rules again. The trouble was, although better than it used to be, his reading wasn't up to tackling complicated jargon. He retrieved a scrunched-up leaflet from the depths of his pocket and smoothed it out. Just looking at it, made his head hurt. It would need a really bright cookie to decipher the tight black print swarming like a battalion of black beetles all over the page. Marigold was his best bet – well worth braving her sharp tongue. He decided to give it a try. A good excuse to see how she was coping. Not well, if this morning was anything to go by.

But first things first. Luke shimmied through the Merricks' kitchen wall and looked under the sink. He grabbed a variety of cleaning products and pulled on Bunny's fur-edged rubber gloves. He had just got going with solvent and scrubbing brush when a car screeched to a halt in the road outside. It was a car that had seen better days.

'Nobody around. Keep her ticking over and I'll get the job finished.' Kevin Jenkins leapt out and strode up the path, spray can in hand. Luke was elbow-deep in soapy water. It was a bizarre picture and the pink rubber gloves did him no favours. Kevin stopped in his tracks and flipped open his camera. 'Mother's little helper?' he sneered. 'A You Tube hit!' But the screen remained blank. No amount of shaking – or swearing – made any difference. 'You got the evil eye or something?'

'Possibly.' Luke fixed Kevin with a cold stare and pointed to the crude Michelin Man. 'Your work, I take it? You're no Banksy, so if I were you, I'd scrub it off before Marigold's father finds it.' He peeled off the gloves and offered them to Kevin. 'And make it quick.'

'Yeah, too true, I'll make it quick alright!' Finger on the nozzle, he pointed the spray can directly into Luke's face. 'Take this, Saddo!' But it didn't work. He rattled the can up and down in frustration. 'Bloody thing!' He was so furious that he went immediately to Plan B and simply threw it in Luke's face.

In his day, Luke had been no mean fielder. He caught the can in one hand and aimed it back at Kevin. A light squeeze on the nozzle and a jet of paint, vivid as blood, spurted all over Kevin's jeans and tee-shirt. Luke found himself enjoying the moment. Pity Marigold wasn't there to share it. More bodyguard than guardian-angel this time round, he reckoned.

'What's keeping you, mate?' A voice from the battered car. 'Can't stop here all day!'

With a last bitter threat that was lost on Luke, Kevin threw himself into the car and slammed the door. Luke smiled, imagining the driver's reaction to his paint-spattered passenger. He struggled back into the pink gloves, dipped his brush into the solvent and did his best to remove the last of the graffiti. Not perfect, he admitted, but not bad for an amateur.

When he had returned the washing-up bowl and gloves to their place under the sink, he stopped off in the neglected garden. A bunch of flowers would be just the thing to soften Marigold's heart, he thought. Women were suckers for flowers. He picked a few of the better-looking specimens and made for the stairs, stopped, went back and took a packet of chocolate biscuits from the worktop – in her half-starved state, Marigold might appreciate these even more than flowers. Biscuits in one hand, flowers in the other, he appeared out of the wall to stand by the side of her bed.

She opened one eye. 'You again?' she said and turned away from him. It wasn't a good beginning. 'I thought you'd done your good deed for the day. You saved me from being run over, so you can go off duty, surely to goodness?'

'I've got a problem,' he said.

'So have I – you.'

Luke put the biscuits on the bed, within easy reach of her hand. 'Try one,' he said eventually. 'You know you want to.'

Marigold did – that was one of the really annoying things about Luke – he knew her better than she did herself, but she was determined to resist.

Luke waved the bunch of flowers at her. 'I brought you these,' he said. 'What should I do with them?'

'Why? Did you think I'd died too?' She felt in no mood to be polite, although she couldn't help being secretly pleased. No-one had ever given her flowers before. She sat up cautiously, protecting her eyes from the glare. Her head was throbbing from the sheer effort of thinking too much. 'Give them here,' she said at last. 'I'll get some water for the poor things.'

She grabbed her dressing gown and staggered down to the kitchen. When she returned with a jug of water, Luke was idly rolling the biscuit packet across the bed. 'Full-fat dark chocolate, this lot,' he said. 'Go on.'

It was too much for Marigold. She tore open the top, offered him a biscuit, then began to stuff them into her mouth, barely taking time to swallow. She was like an addict, eating so fast she spat chocolatey crumbs all over the duvet. Luke watched in amazement.

'That didn't take you long,' he commented, as she aimed the empty packet towards the bin. Like some fussy old lady, she used her forefinger to tidy away the remaining crumbs around her mouth. Then she turned her back to Luke and began to pull on jeans and top.

'You said you had a problem?'

'My reading's not up to much – you know that, of course – so could you help me?' He produced the dog-eared house-rules from the depths of his pocket. 'Try as I might, I can't manage this kind of thing.'

Marigold took the leaflet, smoothed it out and scanned it quickly. 'Looks like a load of gobbledy-gook to me,' she said. 'It's almost as bad as our school brochure.'

'So, what does it say?' Luke was impatient to sort out the rules in his head.

'I don't understand everything – it's too full of words like 'wherefore' and 'hereunto' and 'notwithstanding' to make it an easy read, but the gist of it is that you've got to make a choice and stick to it.'

'Does it say I can't do the dream-thing any more?'

'Not exactly, I think you've got to decide between that and being visible. You can't do both until you're properly dead or something.' If he'd been ordered out of her dreams, it was the best news Marigold had come across in months and her heart lifted. The day-to-day Luke was OK, better than OK in the looks department, but the dreamtime boy was something else. 'There's more – it says here in clause 4.35 that you're not allowed to . . .' She held it up to the window for a better look, turned it upside down, gave up. 'It's no use, the corner's torn off – I can't read the rest.'

Luke began a frantic search through his pockets, with no success – Leslie's car key, a silver button, a piece of string, a rusted knife, but not the smallest scrap of paper.

'Why do they have to make such a big deal of everything?' he complained, the blank angry stare returning.

'Don't blame me, I'm just the messenger.' Marigold handed him back the wrinkled booklet. He balled it into his fist, tossed it into the wastepaper basket, thought better of it and thrust it back into his pocket.

'If I've got to stick to these rules, it's going to make life – if I can still call it that – extremely difficult.' Luke scratched his head in puzzlement.

'How do you mean?'

'Well, if I'm not allowed to keep an eye on you when you're asleep, I won't be able to do my early warning bit.'

'I keep telling you – I'm quite capable of looking after myself, thank you,' she said. If looks could kill, Luke thought – although it was a bit late for that kind of thing. He smiled to himself at his non-joke. Marigold was not amused.

She flopped down on a chair, holding herself in a tight bundle, the chocolate biscuits making a half-digested lump in her chest. How could I have given in to a few biscuits? Where has my famous willpower gone? she berated herself. She began to rock back and forth to some inner rhythm of her own, looking so unhappy that Luke ached to comfort her, to stroke her smooth brown arms, but he didn't dare. She'd have shrugged him off, he was sure of that, yet he alone knew how vulnerable she was, especially today.

CHAPTER SIX

LUKE STOOD BY the open window, trying to decide his next move. The sun still beat down from a tinplate sky, bleaching colour from the dry grass and leaf-heavy trees. There was complete silence outside as though everything had ground to a stop.

He was growing fond of Marigold, infuriating spiky creature that she was, and wanted more than anything else to be able to take proper care of her. His problem? he simply didn't know how. What Danny would have thought of him, he didn't dare imagine. Luke, soppy over a girl? Never. It exasperated him that he couldn't put a finger on the exact nature of the danger that loomed over her. Kevin? Bunny? Something he hadn't yet thought of? Whatever happened, he'd have to keep her onside.

Doing the dream-thing had been a bit of a lark to begin with, staring at Marigold and frightening the life out of her, but he was going soft. It hadn't been so much fun recently. He reluctantly admitted to himself that he might be half in love with her, if that fluttering in the stomach is how love feels. That would be another rule breached, no doubt. If he had to give up the dream-thing, then he'd need to concentrate his energies on re-inhabiting his body full-time, but it was fraught with difficulties. And he needed that passport. Life in the other world would be a dead loss without it.

If he came out as Marigold's full-time boyfriend, he'd have to find a way of living in the real world – and that came with a time limit now that he was officially on the other side. How to cope if he couldn't dive into the dream dimension at will? He'd even been forbidden to use the white cow idea again, although it had seemed a pretty good wheeze at the time.

Along the empty road and into the noonday silence, came the sound of footsteps, tired footsteps by the sound of them and the dragging of something like a laden shopping trolley. It was unusual to hear people passing the Merrick house on foot at any time, let alone anyone pulling along a heavy load on what must surely be the hottest afternoon of the summer, but it wasn't a shopping trolley, as it turned out, it was a suitcase on wheels.

Luke heard the back door squeak open and a woman's voice call out, 'Anyone home?'

Marigold jumped up as though she'd been shot. She dragged her hands through her hair and tumbled downstairs at a rate of knots, all traces of headache gone. 'Mum!' she called. 'Mum!' Thank goodness I can still do invisibility, Luke thought, as he stood in the kitchen doorway staring at the scene from his strange pale eyes.

Marigold's mother, her untidy reddish hair tied up in an assortment of coloured scarves, held her daughter at arm's length. 'Has your dad been starving you?' she asked. 'You look like a rake.'

'It's not like that, Mum, honestly. Dad's been great, it's just that I'm on a diet, I've gone down *two sizes!'*

'I can't say it's done you a lot of good. Nothing a good meal wouldn't sort out.' She sounded thoroughly grumpy – almost like old times, Luke decided, thinking back to his own mother. Perhaps she was just hot and out of sorts, or maybe it was simply the way mothers were, not that he had much recent experience to go on. She sat at the table and looked Marigold up and down, in a guarded kind of way. 'Aren't you going to make a cup of tea for your long-lost mum?'

As Marigold filled the kettle and opened a box of tea-bags, her mother began to take in the changes in the kitchen. She prowled around, lifting and laying unfamiliar storage jars and tea-towels. 'You two have been busy, I see. New mugs?' she asked.

She sat sipping her steaming tea and the cat jumped on to her lap. He turned round a few times, getting to know the smell of her again and settled down, purring like a mini-tiger. It was almost as though she'd never been away. 'Like old times,' she said and a slow smile lit up her face. 'Has your dad come into a lottery win or something?'

'No, it's not that exactly.'

'Well, what?'

Before Marigold could come up with a suitable answer, Dad's car drew up outside. She tried to warn her father, but he bounded up the path and barged through the kitchen door, on fire with excitement. 'Great news, Kid! You'll never believe it!' I'd believe almost anything today, Marigold thought.

Then everything went haywire. Oliver Merrick caught sight of his wife sitting at the table, smiling serenely in that bland way that had so often infuriated him in the past. Eyes popping, he slid to an abrupt stop, like a cartoon cat spying a bulldog. His voice faltered mid-sentence and invisible question marks hung in the air. Her presence was not only unexpected, but totally unwelcome, especially today of all days. His ballooning excitement died as though it had been pricked with a pin. He regrouped and moved slowly to pull out a chair, turn it back to front and sit astride it. He needed to clear his head.

'Molly?' he blustered. 'What brought you back?'

She looked him in the eye. 'Lack of funds, Oliver,' she said. 'I thought you might have worked that out for yourself.'

Marigold's mobile played its silly tune into the stunned silence. She opened the flap. Jocelyn. She had never been so glad to hear from her in her life.

'Got to go,' she said, making for the open door.

'But I thought you weren't feeling too good?' Dad.

'No time to fill me in about what's been happening?' Mum.

Marigold had no intention of stopping to put a gloss on things for either of her parents. They had got themselves into this mess, and it was up to them to sort it out between them, so she upped and ran, out of the house, straight into the arms of Luke. 'Saved by the bell - well, by Joss,' she said, nearly breathless. 'I don't think I can cope any more.'

'It wasn't Jocelyn - it was me,' Luke said. 'I reckoned you'd had enough aggro for one day.'

'I thought you and mobiles didn't mix.'

'We don't as a rule, but I thought it was worth having a go - and it obviously worked, so why worry?'

Marigold hung back for a moment to see what her parents were up to. Their tones were muffled by the closed door, so she couldn't hear the exact words, but it was obvious they were involved in an acrimonious argument. Their voices rose and fell. Like old times indeed. 'They'll be at one another's throats in a minute,' she gasped, all her old fears threatening to overwhelm her. 'Just wait till Mum sees Bunny's stuff in the bathroom, not to mention the frilly cushions on the bed - and the silk dressing gown behind the door - she'll have a fit!'

'Best leave them to it, then,' Luke said.

Marigold's mobile again. 'What's with you?' an aggrieved Jocelyn enquired. 'I've been trying to get hold of you all day. You OK?'

'My mum's come back, so . . .'

'So – it doesn't stop you picking up your phone!' Jocelyn still sounded miffed. Then curiosity got the better of her. 'How's she taking it, the Bunny-thing, I mean?'

'I don't know, I've escaped for the moment, but expect fireworks any time now.'

'Should be fun! Meet me outside Prezzo?'

'On my way. Give me ten minutes.' She turned to Luke, 'Can you make yourself scarce for a couple of hours? I need to speak to Jocelyn on my own.'

'Don't worry, I'll hang about out of sight – but I'd like to be around just in case . . .' He went all serious, his face shadowed by the Boy's cold mask. It sent a momentary shiver along her backbone.

'In case of . . . what?'

He looked puzzled. 'I don't honestly know. They don't let newcomers like me look into the future. But whatever it is, it won't do you any good – I'm sure of that.'

The Moor sweltered in the fierce heat and people struggled with shopping bags to collapse in a heap in the bus shelter or sat slumped on benches under the shade of the trees. Marigold began to wilt, but she was careful not to step on a crack, counting the blocks under her breath as she went. She didn't want to bring another dose of bad luck, especially the way things were going for her at the moment.

Jocelyn waved. She had bagged a sun umbrella, cool drinks ready on the table. Although he left no shadow, Marigold knew that Luke was still at her side. 'Buzz off or Joss will see you. I'll meet you later,' she whispered.

'Promise?'

'Promise.'

Marigold slid into the seat opposite her friend. She grabbed the ice-cold can and swallowed half her drink before she was able to think. 'Thanks,' she said.

'Who was that you were talking to?' Jocelyn asked.

'Me? No-one.'

'Come off it, Mari – I distinctly heard you promise to meet someone. The mysterious boyfriend? Chatting you up for the T-in-the-Park gig, is he?'

'You're imagining things. I've no time for boyfriends or boy-bands or anything else with all that's going on at home.' She would give her eye teeth to be going to the gig, billed as the biggest T-in-the-park event for Cornwall, but it wasn't high on her list of priorities at this particular moment. Besides, she had no-one to go with. Girls didn't count. This was a proper date that meant having a male escort or you were as good as dead as far as your reputation went.

'You'll never guess who's taking me? In his dad's car, I might add!' Jocelyn's face shone pink with conquest.

'No, but you're going to tell me anyway.'

'Harry Stokes.'

'Isn't he in Year 10? I didn't think they knew we existed.'

'Well, they know about me, I made sure of that! Listen . . .'

'I'm all ears.' Might as well get it over with, Marigold thought. She listened with less than half her concentration, most of her mind taken up with what was happening chez Merrick.

'So what do you think?'

'Great.' Marigold sounded so uncharacteristically downbeat that Jocelyn gave in.

'What's with your mum then? I know you're dying to spill the beans.'

She drew her chair forward. Now that she'd squeezed every last drop of gloating out of her date with Harry Stokes, she was ready to share Marigold's drama – her own home-life was tame by comparison. 'Go on, then,' she urged. 'What's been happening?'

Over another can of drink and a cupcake each, Marigold brought Jocelyn up to date. She might have added a touch of colour to the story of her mum's unexpected return, she conceded, but it was substantially true. Her friend was an avid listener. They ordered a slice of chocolate cake to share and a latte each. Marigold couldn't imagine the weight she must have put on in a single afternoon, but it was almost worth it, just to have someone there (who wasn't the ghostly Luke) to listen and sympathise.

Her mobile juddered. Dad. His texting wasn't up to much, *'Trubl need u kid'* but it triggered an immediate response. It wasn't often he admitted to needing her help. She looked at her watch, surprised at the time.

'Dad,' she said. 'I've got to get back. Got to face the music sometime.'

'Do you want me to come with you?' Jocelyn offered.

'No thanks,' Marigold said. 'It's only my mum and dad, after all. They'll probably have sorted it out by now.' But she wasn't sure really, it was only bravado. Anyway, if Luke turned up, as promised, Joss's presence would complicate things.

They went inside to pay at the desk and emerged blinking into the sunshine to find Kevin Jenkins and his mates lounging against the wall. The girls were subjected to some sarcastic wolf-whistling and a few unfavourable personal comments. Pretending to be deep in conversation, they did their best to ignore it. 'The boyfriend's made himself scarce, I see,' Kevin said.

Jocelyn wore her 'told-you-so' face. Marigold felt trapped, so she attacked her antagonist head-on. 'Drop dead!' she snapped at him. She was aware of the half-dead Luke hovering in the vicinity, so it wasn't the most appropriate threat in the circumstances. She could hear a snort of smothered laughter, so presumably he didn't mind.

'No law that says we can't hang around here, is there?' The lads began to wheel round the girls, menace in their every movement. Then Kevin edged away from the others and grabbed Marigold by the arm. 'I've got a proposition for you, Bird,' he said, pulling her to one side.

Bird? She shook him off. 'Like what?'

'Fancy coming to the Heligan gig with me?'

She tossed her hair back in the approved teenage manner. 'You must be joking!' But this was a first. Kevin Jenkins had never before given her a passing glance, unless to use her for verbal target practice. She couldn't help just the merest feel-good smirk crossing her face. Mind you, he had a nerve after plastering their front door with his horrible fattist graffiti. She shook off his hand and ostentatiously dusted her arm.

'Go on,' Dave, one of the others said. 'Old Kev fancies you rotten. Didn't you know?' In spite of herself, Marigold blushed. 'You're not a bad-looking bird these days. It's them skimpy tops you've started wearing.'

Jocelyn hauled her friend away. 'It's obvious she doesn't want to be seen with you lot. Scram!' But they weren't about to give in so easily. They circled the two girls, whistling at them. It was strangely intimidating. 'Go on Bird, give the guy a break!'

Suddenly, for no apparent reason, they seemed to lose control of their cycles until riders and machines lay in a mangled heap on the pavement, wheels spinning.

Jocelyn couldn't believe what she was seeing. 'I've no idea what happened, but that's the funniest thing I've seen in years!' she spluttered. Luke, thought Marigold, bang on cue.

'Come on,' she said. 'I've got to get back. Let's go while the going's good.'

Jocelyn was torn. Although part of her was reluctant to give up on the Merrick drama, her more sensible side was secretly glad to catch the 38 and get on home to the stodgy safety of her own family. She hugged herself at the thought of her date with Harry, now that was her idea of excitement. And she had still to decide what to wear. 'Sure you'll be OK?' she called, but her friend had gone.

There was an air of uncanny calm when Marigold let herself into the house. No shouting, no crying – in fact, it was so quiet that she began to think that her parents had made their escape into the sunset hand-in-hand, like in the cinema, leaving her alone to pick up the pieces. But it was an impossible dream and she knew it. After all, just minutes previously, Dad had left that frantic message on her mobile. She had to do something about it – and fast!

Like a cat burglar in her own house, she crept upstairs and silently opened one door after another. No-one about, so she retreated to her own room. There she found her mother standing on a chair, humming under her breath, as she stuck stray silver stars to the ceiling.

'Your diamonds are falling from the sky,' she said, calm as you like. 'Pass me up the tube of Fix-it, please love.'

'Mum?' Marigold was wary. 'Are you staying?'

'Why not? It's my house.'

'Yes but, how does Dad feel about it? And what about . . . ?'

'Hamster? Or whatever that ridiculous woman is called – I'm not worried about her!'

When Marigold's phone rang again, it made her jump. She answered, heard the strangled sound of sobbing, under control, but all the more devastating for that. Fathers don't cry, as a general rule.

'Dad?' she said, but the line went dead. 'Where's Dad?' she asked aloud.

'No idea. I don't know what to make of him, I really don't – he's been bawling like a baby all afternoon.' Her mother was nonchalant, still busy with the silver stars.

A clearing of the throat in the doorway – Luke. He stood just out of sight and beckoned her over. 'I think you'd better come, Goldielocks. The grapevine tells me we've got a problem on our hands.' All this in a stage whisper.

'Dad?' Luke nodded, taking the stairs down two at a time.

She bolted after him, panting with effort. Her mother's voice, unhurried, unworried, echoed through the silent house. 'Going out again, Marigold? Always gadding about, you are – your father's influence, I suppose.' A deep sigh followed, but Marigold was well on her way by this time.

'I wish they still issued us with wings, like in the old days,' Luke complained. 'We sure could use them on this kind of mission.' He grabbed Marigold by the hand and somehow they began to move along in that mysterious free-floating dream-thing fashion, not quite touching the ground with their feet. Not that she had much time to think about it, she was too worried about her father.

'You do know where he is?' she asked.

Luke, in the Boy mode, treated her to a stony stare. 'Yeah, but you won't like it. How's your head for heights?'

'So-so.'

'Well, you're going to need it.' In no time at all, they had space-hopped their way along the A39 to Truro and ended up in the town centre. Certainly a lot faster than taking the bus, Marigold conceded. Tourists and shoppers alike, stopped and stared at her as she raced past. Luke they ignored, of course.

'Must be those new 'heelies' or whatever they call them,' they commented, as they tried to make sense of her unusual mode of travel.

'All the rage, these days.' Satisfied, the onlookers nodded and hurried about their business.

Marigold tried to slow Luke down. 'This is the Cathedral,' she said. 'Dad doesn't believe in all that church stuff. We won't find him in here.' She looked at the three tall spires piercing the skyline.

'Trust me,' Luke said, as he bypassed the shadowy entrance. 'No time for the stairway – we'd better take the fast lane. It will land me in more trouble, I expect, but needs must. Don't look down, Goldielocks.' And with that, they were abseiling hand-over-hand up the front face of the Cathedral, to the consternation of by-standers on the ground. Close-up, the nooks and crannies in great pointed spires gave her the shivers.

'Look at that stupid girl!' a voice from the street. 'What does she think she's doing?'

A crowd had gathered in the square below. Some were busy on their mobiles, a few taking photographs, others dialling 999. High Cross had come to a complete halt.

She found her father hanging over the low stone wall, gazing down at the town spread below. He was wearing an unfamiliar high visibility vest. 'Some view!' he greeted her, his voice calm, although his face betrayed the smudge of tears. Dad crying? It was too much.

'Dad! Are you OK?' Then, annoyance overcoming fear, 'What on earth are you doing up here?'

'Just thinking.' He leaned further out.

'Well, you've chosen a really stupid place to do it. And how the blazes did you make it to the roof? They've got security people crawling all over the place.'

'A yellow jacket will get you anywhere!' He squeezed her hand, smiled down at her, briefly pleased with his ingenuity.

A sudden breeze caught Marigold unawares and blew her hair over her eyes. As she pushed it away, she caught sight of her father looking out across the town. She grabbed hold of his jacket, worried for a moment that he might jump. She had a memory of her dad doing the very same thing when, as a toddler, she had ventured too near the river. It was as though they had changed places.

'I really need to talk to you, Kid.' He'd gone all solemn again, as he fumbled in his pocket and removed an official-looking envelope. It flapped in the wind.

'Problems?'

'Big problems . . . but you're too young to understand.'

'Try me.' She looked round to see if Luke was listening, but he had melted into the tower wall. Whatever it was, she'd have to sort this out on her own.

Luke hadn't simply done his usual disappearing trick. It was more urgent. As predicted, he'd been called away by the Voice. 'Get your act together, Boy,' it said. 'You haven't got a lot of time left in the Other Place.'

'I'm doing my best.'

'Well, your best isn't good enough. You want to join us Up Here, don't you?' Luke nodded. 'To get a passport, you need A+ in everything, absolutely everything - understand?' The Voice sounded exasperated. 'It's all in the rules!' A queue of assorted characters had formed in front of him, some elderly people, a little girl holding a teddy, soldiers still in uniform (from different sides, by the look of it) and a couple of teenagers. A bored official stamped their papers, counting them on a clicker as they passed into the Presence - only Luke was barred. 'No papers, no entry,' a burly minder said.

'Yeah, but I don't understand – how do I qualify?' Luke was reluctant to leave without getting the mission straight in his own mind.

'Use your brain – if you still have one!' the Voice barked. 'Your job is to save that girl, before your time runs out. Have I made myself clear?'

'Crystal clear,' Luke said. 'But I haven't a clue about where to start. Of course, I'm ready to look after her body and soul . . .'

'Body and soul! Listen to the boy!' The Voice spluttered with laughter. 'You don't have a body – and the way you're going on, your soul won't be up to much either!' He was in stitches at his own joke and everyone in the queue smiled politely in response.

'Now, get on with it, Boy. Can't you see I've got a crowd of newcomers to interview?'

Luke mumbled his thanks and was on the point of leaving when the Voice whispered a final piece of advice in his ear, 'Don't get any silly ideas about falling for the girl – that would be a complete waste of time,' and chuckling to himself, he dismissed Luke from his presence.

CHAPTER SEVEN

UP ON THE tower, Oliver Merrick put a protective arm round his daughter's shoulders. 'You're a bit on the skinny side these days,' he observed. 'All sharp corners, like the proverbial bunch of keys.'

'Mum said the same thing, more or less.'

'Mum?' He sighed. 'Your mum's upset the apple-cart good and proper, she has.' He was thoughtful, no longer sounding quite like the distraught man who had left a message on Marigold's phone. 'I didn't imagine she'd ever come back, Kid, I really didn't.'

'She seems to think she's home for good.'

'That's just it – I don't know what to do – Bunny's part of my life, especially now.'

'Now?'

Her father took a deep breath. 'Now that there might be a baby on the way . . .' He looked cautiously at Marigold to see how she was taking the news.

'A baby?'

'I was so excited, desperate to tell you all about it – then your mother turned up out of the blue! She's a bad dream come true, she is.' Her dad thumped his fist on the handrail. 'Just when everything was going so well . . .' Marigold detected a certain shiftiness in his manner. 'Well, almost everything – I can't honestly say that Bunny is over the moon about the baby. And your mother is positively livid!'

'I'm not surprised.'

'Then this morning, on top of everything else, a letter from the bank.' He waved it in front of her, thought better of it, and stuffed it back into his pocket. 'It usually brings bad tidings, but nothing like this – we're into overdraft, and then some – not sure how it's happened . . .' Words tumbled out, tripping over one another at times. 'I thought we had plenty of cash, not a lot, you know, but enough . . . I'm sorry, Kid, so sorry. I didn't realise what was happening – you know what I'm like with money, come easy, go easy.'

He looked so stricken that Marigold felt that *she* should comfort *him*. The role-reversal was complete. She reached for his hand, thick-fingered, firm and strong like it had always been. For a moment, she felt almost reassured.

'Don't worry, Dad. I expect we can sort it out. There's been a mistake, I'm sure.' But in her head, she began to wonder about Bunny's place in all this. Of course, Dad's card had taken a hit the day they had gone shopping-crazy and there must have been other occasions she knew nothing about – the tasteful pottery, the hand-made jewellery, the expensive restaurants all crowded into her mind.

'Dad?' This was going to be difficult. 'Dad, is Bunny still using your card?'

'*Our* card,' he corrected her. 'Of course she is. We're partners, what is it you lot say – an item?' He promptly went into defence mode. 'I trust Bunny absolutely, if that's what you're getting at. It's your mother's unexpected arrival that's doing my head in.' He let out a strange sound, somewhere between a snort and a sigh. 'The Bank's got things all wrong, you know what they're like. It would happen now, when we need the money urgently.' He gripped the top of the wall. 'I'll just have to borrow, there's nothing else for it.'

'Why?' Marigold ventured. 'Why now?'

He father looked bleak. 'Bunny's operation.'

'Operation?'

'Well, she says a baby won't fit into her lifestyle . . .'

'You mean an abortion?'

'I'm desperately trying to persuade her to keep it, really I am. I thought it was going to be wonderful, you, me, Bunny and a new baby. She was none too keen in the first place, to tell the truth, but she knew how thrilled I felt and I thought, hoped, we'd moved on.' He went quiet, thinking. 'But now that your mother's back, I reckon there's no way she'll be prepared to go ahead, so we need the money – and the Bank insists our account's in the red. I just can't think where we go from here . . .' Marigold was terrified that he was going to cry again. She couldn't bear it, not those dry coarse sobs she'd heard on the phone.

She had never given much thought to the pros and cons of abortion. It was something she'd read about and, as a paid-up feminist, she was all for it, but the reality was a different matter. She was unprepared for the effect it was having on her father – the baby's father too – now that was a new thought. A baby in the family would certainly have been an interesting prospect.

She became aware that Luke was trying to get a word in. Marigold had almost forgotten about him. He tried to take her hand, but she shook him off. Luke would be sure to have an opinion, but right now, the need to console her dad was taking all her concentration.

'A baby sister, that would be quite something,' she said, sounding as upbeat as possible in the circumstances. 'Or a brother – I could put up with that! Come on, Dad. Let's go back and talk to Bunny. Maybe it's not too late.'

'OK, Kid. Just give me a minute.' Marigold left him to think over his options and stood leaning against the wall. Everyone in the crowd seemed to be gazing up at her. Then a police car swept into the square. People pointed, hushed.

Looking down, Marigold began to get that familiar flaky feeling, sickness in her throat, emptiness behind her eyes. She began to count the gargoyles round the spire – anything to calm her down – but they ran out at twenty seven. I know, she thought, I'll count the people in the crowd below, so she climbed on to the first rung to get a better view.

'The girl!' one of the by-standers shouted, 'She's going to jump! Can't somebody do something?' The idea both terrified and attracted her – it would be so easy, just one little step into the air and her problems would be over. Cue for Luke to take action, Marigold thought, as she was grabbed by the arm. But Luke was nowhere to be seen. It was her father who had dragged her back.

'What the hell do you think you're doing?'

Before she could explain, a policeman puffed to the top of the staircase. 'Everything OK?' he gasped, emerging from the low doorway.

'Yes, thanks. My daughter and I are just enjoying the view. Truro's a pretty amazing city seen from this angle, don't you think, Constable?' Oliver Merrick was out to prove how cool he was.

'A lot of people were dead worried, sir. Called us out on a 999, they did.'

'I'm so sorry if we've caused any trouble. I find that all this puts my problems into perspective.' He waved at the scene below.

'Well, if you're sure, sir,' the policeman was torn – it would take forever to write up his notes. He looked at his watch, 'I'm due to clock off in ten minutes.' His mobile buzzed and he whispered into his collar. 'Spoke too soon,' he said. 'Duty calls.' And he was off, sprinting downstairs. A few minutes later, they saw him sink into the passenger seat as the police car sped off.

Father and daughter slowly made their way down to ground level and the crowd, finding the excitement over, began to melt away. Luke, in invisible mode, met them at the iron-studded door.

'Goldielocks,' his voice was urgent. 'Listen, we haven't much time.'

On the evening news, the presenter wore his bad-news face. *'Police divers have found the body of a teenage boy. It has not yet been identified, but it is rumoured to be that of a missing runaway from the children's home in Cannington. It is said that the boy thumbed a lift in a lorry that went into the river more than three months ago. The driver was rescued, but so far nothing has been seen of the youth.'*

Luke tried and failed to escape the Voice whose three words, 'Now or never!' were echoing through his head. I wish they'd give me more of a clue, he thought, taking a chance and hot-footing it to Bunny's place. Bingo! He found Marigold, alone and white-faced, in the immaculate kitchen. She was retching over the sink. The sounds of a battle royal reverberated from the living room.

In his silent way, he surprised the girl by standing behind her and touching her hair with the tips of his fingers. She didn't jump, simply turned to lean against him. Luke shuddered, not understanding the feeling that shot through him. Is this what being in love is like? he wondered. But it's not on, he knew that. 'You look pretty rough,' he said.

'I bet I look tons better than you do, now they've dredged you up from the shore.'

'How do you know?'

'You've been on the telly – top-billing on West Country news.'

'So that's why the Voice is getting so worked up?'

He found a glass and filled it with water. He put it to Marigold's lips. 'Gently does it,' he said. 'Don't down it in one gulp.'

She took no more than a sip before throwing up once more. 'I'll be OK in a minute,' she said, wiping her face with a piece of kitchen roll. 'Honestly, I will. There's no need to hang around.'

'Sure?' The Voice was becoming more demanding than ever. There was no way Luke could drown it out. 'Urgent call,' he said.

'Looks like I've got to get going, but I'll be back.' He touched her lightly on the cheek and disappeared.

Luke screwed up his courage, thinking he'd been called away for a briefing on 'How to be a Hero and Get your Passport Free!' No such luck. Instead, he found himself in charge of a squalling baby. He had never seen one close up before and hadn't the foggiest notion of how to cope with it. He jiggled it up and down, hoping that the noise would stop. But, no. The baby simply upped its crying another notch. Then, from the other end, it soaked Luke's only tee-shirt.

'What on earth am I supposed to do with you?' he asked, holding the tiny creature against his shoulder. A brainwave. Danny knew all there was to know about babies. His mother had five of them, one a year after Danny himself, regularly as clockwork. But, how to get in touch with him? And could he risk making a sudden appearance? He was presumed drowned, after all! Maybe that was a bad idea.

He rocked the baby about a bit and patted it on the back, trying hard to remember the words of songs his grandmother had sung to him when he was little. 'Twinkle, twinkle little star . . .' he sang in a hoarse voice – singing was never his strong point – but he couldn't remember what came next, so had to improvise, 'trapped inside a marmalade jar.'

'Not good, but not bad either.' He couldn't quite place the voice. 'Come on, hand him over.' Soft rounded arms reached out for the baby who in some magic way, immediately quietened down. Perhaps he felt safe. Perhaps it's all to do with experience, Luke thought. 'Twinkle, twinkle little star, how I wonder what you are . . .' a woman's voice had taken up the song where he'd left off . . . 'Up above the world so high, like a diamond in the sky.'

She smoothed a strand of damp hair away from her face and Luke was able to have a better look. 'Mum,' he said. 'You didn't make it?'

''Fraid not.' At that moment a call echoed round the hall. It came from a loudspeaker hidden on the edge of a silver cloud. 'Luke Appleton to the Throne Room!' The Voice sounded even more regal than usual – and more threatening – if that were possible.

'Sorry, Mum. Got to go. OK if I leave the baby with you? I'll fill you in on things soon, I promise.'

'Kiss for your old mum,' she pleaded. That was going a bit too far, so Luke made do with giving her a swift pat on the head. Her curls sprung up against his hand, just as Marigold's had done when he ruffled her hair in Bunny's kitchen. 'On you go, my boy. I don't appear to have lost my touch just yet,' she said. She sounded very pleased with herself. The baby, all toothless gums, smiled up at his mum and she smiled back.

'You took your time,' the Voice complained as Luke puffed into his presence.

'Sorry, sir.'

'You're not going to go through all that sorry stuff again, I hope.'

'No, sir. Sorry, sir.'

The Voice went quiet. Luke shuffled his feet, wishing he could see a face. He thought he probably looked something like his old headmaster, complete with horn-rimmed spectacles. 'Listen here, Boy,' he said at last. 'You've messed up again – and now they've found your body, you're running out of time. This is your last chance if you want to join us up here. Sort that girl out once and for all.'

'I'm on my way, sir.' He hesitated. 'How long have I got?'

A deep sigh. 'Do I have to spell it out? Now your body's been identified, you get to dream-walk once and once only – so you've got to make it work. I guess you've got . . . another 48 hours or so. Understood?'

Luke gulped, nodded. 'Understood.' So what Marigold had said was true. They'd found him – or what was left of him. He didn't want to think about his body lying on a slab, who does?

'And another thing, if you want that passport, be back here on the dot of Saturday midnight . . . not a minute later.' With that threat ringing in his ears, Luke promised himself he was up for whatever it took.

'No worries, sir. I'll be there.'

'That's the spirit!' An off-the-cuff remark that rang much too true – he'd been growing lighter, taking on a more ghost-like quality ever since his body had been found. With a shrug of the shoulders, he accepted that his spell in the world below would be short, so he'd better make the most of it. With that thought in his head, he shot back to be with the girl who might have become a *girlfriend* if only he'd had more time. If only . . .

Marigold felt a familiar tap on her shoulder. 'Let's get you safely out of here, Goldielocks.'

'I'm not going anywhere, not without Dad – and he's still tied up as you can see.'

The argument from the sitting room was still going strong, the words rising and falling. 'It's all your fault, Ollie. You should have been more careful. I trusted you!'

'My fault? *My fault?'*

'You know I never wanted to be lumbered with a kid . . .'

'Lumbered? I'd call it blessed . . .'

'Well, tough luck, Ollie. You're too late. No need for nappies, late nights – no need for you, come to think. Not now.'

'You mean . . . ?'

'Yup, the deed is over and done with. Not something I enjoyed, but it's no longer my problem – nor yours – any more!' The adults, much too intent on getting the better of one another, had completely forgotten Marigold. She overheard every bitter word from her place at the kitchen sink.

'The baby's dead,' she whispered, shuddering into Luke's shoulder. 'We're too late.'

Luke's mind raced. So that's what the baby thing's all about – he must be Marigold's nearly-brother. 'I know, I know,' he soothed. Marigold was startled out of her tears.

'You *know?* How can you?' she protested, her voice rising. 'You're one crazy guy. Why should I listen to a word you say?' He didn't try to defend himself, simply drew the spiky creature into his arms, rocked and patted her like the baby he'd tried to comfort earlier.

'Ssh! Ssh! Don't cry, Goldielocks. Please don't cry.' He found that she fitted neatly under his chin. Now that's a really nice sensation, he thought, loving the warmth of her body so close to his. He wondered if he dare kiss her. That would feel even better, he was sure, but he guessed he'd gone quite far enough. Marigold didn't strike him as the kissing type. True to form, she straightened up and shrugged him away.

Conscious that he might be called away at any time, Luke searched in his pockets to find something to give this girl, a keepsake to prove that once he'd been real. His fingers clenched round a car key, Leslie's car key. It was an important part of his old life, but useless if he was on the fast lane to the Upstairs world.

'Take this, Goldielocks – not much of a present, but the best I can do at this moment.' He pressed the key into her hand and kissed her lightly on the cheek. It felt soft as a petal, just as her knew it would. He shivered.

Marigold's father had flopped on to the settee. Like a freshly-caught fish, he was gasping for air. 'And you didn't think I had any say in it? It was my baby too – or didn't you think of that?'

'Nothing to do with you – it was *my* kid and I got rid of it. All things considered, I wouldn't mind putting my feet up for an hour. It wasn't simply a matter of shelling peas, you know. So . . .' Bunny walked slowly to the door and opened it wide. 'Good-bye, Ollie. Nice knowing you.'

'But I love you.' He groped for her hand, a pathetic attempt to connect, but Bunny was having none of it.

She swatted him away. 'It's over, Ollie. Don't you get it?' Marigold couldn't bear to watch her father. He seemed to shrivel into himself as he rose and, without another word of protest, shuffled towards the door. They had both forgotten her existence.

But Marigold didn't intend to let Bunny off the hook. She shook herself upright, disdain written all over her face. 'Think you're something special, do you?' she spat. 'Well, let me tell you, you're not fit to black my father's boots!' It was an over-dramatic childish thing to say, but it made her feel a lot better.

'Atta girl!' said a voice in her ear. She stood tall and strode past a startled Bunny, Luke invisible in her slipstream.

'That's it then,' Marigold's father commented as they drove away from Bunny's flat. 'I'm a stupid old man trying to behave like a twenty-something. I'm sorry, Kid, so sorry.' Marigold couldn't trust herself to say anything, so she gave his free hand a reassuring squeeze. There was a tense silence in the car as they made their way home. She was glad of Luke's reassuring presence hovering somewhere in the back of the car.

As they drew up, they were met with an appetising smell wafting from the kitchen.

'Chilli con carne OK for everyone?' Marigold's mother was wielding a wooden spoon over a pan bubbling on the cooker. She smiled at her husband and daughter, looking for all the world as though she'd never been away. 'By the way,' she said, 'a friend of yours has been hanging around all afternoon, seems keen, says he's your boyfriend. What's his name? Colin, Callum, Kevin . . . something like that? Hasn't given me a moment's peace.'

'I knew you had a boyfriend, felt it in my water.'

'Dad! Kevin Jenkins's no boyfriend of mine!'

'He wants to take you out for tea, apparently. Where was it again? Somewhere in the park? Strange, I thought you'd outgrown the park. And he's talking about dancing a jig.'

Her mother hadn't changed a bit. She only listened to half of any conversation. 'Not jig, Mum. Gig. In the Lost Gardens – a T-in-the-Park gig.'

'That's exactly what I said.' She piled rice on to three plates and put the chilli into a dish in the middle of the table. It smelt wonderful. 'And I want no nonsense about diets,' she said, scowling at her daughter. 'So, what's the latest? I need to get up to speed with what's been happening. Anything interesting?' She had completely morphed back into the scatty mother she'd always been, looking from one face to the other, beady-eyed as a bird returning to its nest. Marigold couldn't think where to start and didn't dare glance at her father who was apparently concentrating hard on the food in front of him.

'Not much,' Marigold said, lying through her teeth.

'Got rid of the Hamster, have you, Oliver? A sensible move if I may say so.' Marigold's dad laid down his fork and cleared his throat, ready to confess all.

'I've been very foolish, Molly. But, you see, I was lonely . . .' Her mum cocked her head and pursed her lips. It was a gesture Marigold recognised of old. Things were about to go pear-shaped once again.

At that precise moment, the clock jumped off the wall. It was a pretty china thing, with a pattern round the edge, one they'd brought back from a holiday in Spain, a clock they barely noticed any more. It teetered in the air, somersaulted and chimed as it crashed to the floor. Marigold counted the chimes. Thirteen. Clocks don't strike thirteen, she told herself, certainly not of their own volition. There was only one answer.

'What the blazes . . . ?' Dad said.

'I swear there's a ghost in this house!' Never had her mum spoken a truer word.

Under cover of the clearing-up kerfuffle, Marigold whispered some advice. 'Don't say any more, Dad,' she whispered. 'It'll blow over.' There was a heavy silence, broken only by the sound of shattered crockery being swept away.

'I never really liked that old clock anyway. It's always slow – or fast, I can't remember which.' Typical Mum. When the bin lid slammed down on the last shards, she sat back down at the table. She laid a hand on her husband's and smiled one of her goofy smiles. 'Let's put it down to late wild-oats, shall we?' She'd obviously decided to let by-gones be by-gones. 'Strawberries and cream, anyone?' she asked.

A ring of the bell, followed immediately by an impatient knock on the front door. People rarely rang the Merricks' door bell. Surprised, Marigold got up to see who it was. 'It must be the boyfriend,' her mother said in a stage whisper. 'What did I tell you? I knew he'd be back!'

Sure enough, Kevin lounged in the porch.

'What do you want?' Marigold didn't attempt to sound polite.

'Didn't your mum say? You know the T-in-the-Park thing in Heligan tomorrow night? Fancy coming with me?'

'I most certainly do not!'

'Come on Bird. I can get tickets. Do the thing properly.' He looked her up and down with a calculating gaze. 'You're quite fanciable these days, you know.'

'So?' It gave her just a smidgin of pride to be called fanciable by the likes of Kevin Jenkins, but she had no intention of letting on. 'Well, that's too bad – because I don't fancy you!'

'You mean you're going to sit at home watching telly with the Aged Parents after waiting yonks for a gig like this to come to Cornwall? Get a life!'

'Get lost!' She tried to close the door, but Kevin stuck his foot in the gap. He leered at her. He wasn't used to girls turning him down.

'You'll be sorry, Bird. You'll see.'

Truth to tell, Marigold would love to have gone. The gig was a one-off and *The Bo-Jangles,* the boy-band of all boy-bands, was to be the star attraction. She could imagine the lights, the ear-bending noise, the sheer excitement. If only it hadn't been dead-beat Kevin. It was a stand-off. She watched him from under her lids. I suppose he's not really too bad-looking, she thought. Pity he's such an utter nerd. 'Sure, Bird?' It was Kevin's last shot.

'Absolutely! Now, clear off!'

'Stuff you!' He slouched down the path, hands deep in the pockets of his half-mast jeans. In spite of everything, Marigold felt a twinge of disappointment. Maybe she should call him back. Not that she rated him, of course, although Kevin was regarded as a bit of a catch among some of the girls. Not Joss, of course, she thinks he's gross. So perhaps it's just as well.

'Make up your mind, Marigold. Either close that door or invite the boyfriend in to meet us,' her mother called. Marigold didn't answer. She stumbled upstairs, at war with herself. This is what she had wanted, T-in-the-Park, in Heligan's Lost Gardens to be exact, was a once in a lifetime event - and the girls had been talking about nothing else for weeks, planning what to wear, what to do with their hair and now she had turned down her only chance. Great to be upsides with Jocelyn for once - although a Y8 Kevin didn't come anywhere near a Y10 Harry. She imagined Jocelyn swanning along with the delectable Harry in tow. Life was a pig! She curled up on top of her bed.

'D'you want these strawberries or not?' Her mother was shouting from the bottom of the stair. 'You could do with a bit of fattening up.'

'She's right, you know.' Luke's familiar voice. 'Go on, Goldielocks. Give your mum a break.'

'Since when did you get to be so knowledgeable about mothers?' Marigold's attempt at sarcasm washed over him. But the thought of the first sweet strawberries of the season made her mouth water and lured her downstairs. 'OK, OK, I'm on my way.' She slammed the door in Luke's face, not that it made much difference. Doors didn't figure in his current incarnation, but it gave her a good feeling.

Peace had broken out at the Merrick tea-table. It was amazing what a freshly-cooked meal and some new season's strawberries could do. Dad had opened a bottle of white wine, cold from the fridge. 'To welcome you back, Molly. We're a family again!' They clinked glasses. Even Marigold had been included, not that she was a great fan of wine. She stole a glance at Dad's face and thought how sad he looked under the bonhomie. Was it the loss of the baby, or Bunny, or both? Her mother took no notice and burbled on about how good it was to be home.

The doorbell chimed again. 'I bet it's the boyfriend. He obviously isn't taking 'No' for an answer. Invite him in this time.' Marigold shot to the door and wrenched it open.

'You again?'

But the boy who stood on the doorstep wasn't Kevin. It was Luke, a real-live Luke brandishing tickets for the Heligan gig

Marigold thought she was seeing things and simply stood like a lemon in the doorway. Barely two minutes ago he'd been his shadowy self talking to her on the landing.

'You don't know the problems I had getting these.' He seemed very pleased with himself.

'You're not serious?'

In a flash, Luke's eyes turned to dream-thing stones and he spoke slowly and carefully, as though she didn't understand English. 'I am – formally – inviting – you – to – partner – me – at the T-in-the-Park thing tomorrow evening. Will that do?' He'd speeded up by this time. 'You'd love to go, wouldn't you?'

'Course I would, but I can hardly go with you. Aren't you officially dead?'

'Not exactly, not yet. I'll tell you all about it later. Please, Goldielocks. It's the one and only chance we'll get.' His eyes grew gentle as he reached out to touch her face with spider-fingertips. In spite of herself, she shivered with delight. 'Aren't you going to ask me in to meet your folks?'

'Don't be so utterly stupid! I can hardly introduce them to a ghost!'

'Look, I promise I won't do my disappearing trick this time. I can act quite civilised when I put my mind to it.' Reluctantly, she nodded him inside.

'You won't let me down?'

'I won't.' He put his warm hand in the small of her back and followed Marigold into the kitchen.

'Mum, Dad, this is Luke.' They were obviously impressed. No wonder, Luke was tall, fair and exceedingly handsome, perfect boyfriend material – only the eyes were disconcerting.

'Pleased to meet you,' he said, reaching out to shake their hands. It turned out that he was adept at small-talk, moving the conversation easily from garden to weather, from pop-music to books he had recently read. Marigold's mother couldn't contain her curiosity.

'And how did you two meet?' she asked.

Both replied at once. 'At school,' Marigold.

'In the library,' Luke. He swiftly amended his explanation to, 'In the school library.'

'I can tell you're a scholar. You've got that look about you.' Marigold's mother smiled benignly at this unlikely blond god that her Ugly Duckling of a daughter had so unexpectedly produced.

'Off to university soon, I expect?' Her dad was equally intrigued by the young man. 'Decided what you want to study?'

'Not absolutely certain, sir. Philosophy perhaps – if I have the time.' Luke said airily.

'Like to join us in a glass of wine, young man?' Dad asked.

Luke consulted his watch. 'Sorry Mr Merrick . . .'

'Oliver,' Dad chipped in.

'Things to do, I'm sure you'll understand. OK if I pick you up about eight tomorrow evening, Marigold?' She nodded, speechless for once. 'Nice you have met you, Mr – Oliver – and Mrs Merrick.' And he did another round of hand-shaking.

'Did I pass muster?' he asked Marigold as they made for the door.

'You got an A* for that performance,' she said. He squeezed her hand.

'See you at eight – all glammed up, yes?'

'I'll do my best.' A last cheeky grin in Marigold's direction and he vanished. Pfff – into the sunshine, like a mirage. Hope he doesn't do this tomorrow night, she thought.

Back indoors, Marigold was conscious of Mum looking at her with new eyes. She couldn't help smirking a bit as she helped with the washing-up.

'Got something decent to wear?' her mother asked, plunging a plate into the suds. It was the first time ever she'd taken any interest in Marigold's clothes.

'I should blooming well hope so,' her dad said, as if to himself, 'considering the bashing my card has taken recently.'

'That's not fair, blaming me, Dad – and you know it!' a fierce whisper in her father's general direction.

'I suppose you did get some help.' That was probably the last time she ever heard him refer to Bunny, even obliquely. He pushed at his glasses and sighed a deep impossible sigh as he spread bank statements across the table. 'Bad news, bad news,' he muttered.

Any other time, Marigold would have been at his side, calculator in hand to offer help. Not today, however. She couldn't wait to look through her stuff and decide what to wear. This was a first. No wonder the other girls thought her odd. Maybe this is how they feel about clothes all the time.

As Marigold edged her way towards the door, her imagination full of skirts and tops, Mum found Bunny's fur-trimmed rubber gloves hiding beneath the sink. Bad timing. Marigold almost stopped breathing as she waited for the explosion. But it didn't come. Making sure that Dad was watching every move, her mother picked up the gloves between thumb and forefinger, held them at arms' length and dropped them one by one, into the bin. Then slowly and carefully she washed and dried her hands as though they'd been contaminated by a deadly virus. She said nothing, but the straightening of her shoulders and the toss of her head gave her away. It was time for her to get down to business, Bunny-business. She dug out a black bag.

'I'm going to clear all that stuff out of the bathroom before I pass out from the pong. I don't know how you two have put up with it.'

A few minutes later, she marched outside, black bag swinging from her hands. 'I've never come across such rubbish - and in my own bathroom!' Marigold thought of the pretty little pots of rainbow nail varnish, the spray perfumes, the lip gloss. It would be a pity to waste everything, she decided, so she waited until she heard Mum's footsteps on the stairs to scuttle out of the back door and search through the contents of the bin.

What was it they said, 'Waste not, want not'? Marigold stowed Bunny's cosmetics in her old toy drawer. Even her mother wouldn't think of looking in there. It might make it easier for her to get 'glammed up', as Luke had requested.

She lay on top of the duvet in a glorious daydream, imagining herself transformed like some latter day Cinderella ready for her date - and with the undoubtedly handsome Luke. Just one fly in the ointment - what if he didn't turn up? What if he disappeared into thin air? That would be a dream turned nightmare, the dream-thing in broad daylight.

CHAPTER EIGHT

LUKE SAT ON the fence at the bottom of the garden keeping a wary eye on the Merrick household. Everything appeared to be calm and ordered. No prima-donna histrionics. The car didn't move from its parking place. The garden was left to its own devices. This was Luke's big moment and he knew it. He felt twitchy, jumped a mile at the smallest sound.

For better or worse, he held Marigold's fate in his hands. Something bad would happen to her in the next 48 hours, he felt it in his bones. His previous efforts had simply been pretty feeble try-outs for the big event, so he tried to gear himself up for a final showdown.

Sure, a couple of times he had saved her from a mauling by the Y8 bullies and he was glad he'd been around when she was being humiliated by the Bunny-woman – the wine-spilling trick still brought a smile of triumph to his face. But that was chicken-feed, there must be more to this caring stint than that. Trust him to be off-duty when she'd been about to jump from the Cathedral roof. He'd have enjoyed playing the knight in shining armour on that occasion, but her old man got all the glory instead.

Feeling redundant for the first time since he walked out of the dream-thing and met Marigold for real, he toyed with every possible scenario, burning buildings, a car chase, a lightning strike, each one more fanciful than the last. Aware that he was no hero, he just hoped he'd be up to it when the call came.

Sitting around waiting for something to happen wasn't Luke's style. In fact, it bored him rigid, so he tried to get his head together for tomorrow's big event, mentally ticking off his to-do's. If he wasn't to let Marigold down, he'd have to get himself kitted out in suitable gear. And, of course, transport of some kind was going to be of prime importance. Heligan was a fair step, 25 miles or so, he reckoned. He was a good driver, he'd practised in the old wild days when he was bumming around, before he'd ever set foot in Cannington – the fact that he was under-age and didn't have a licence needn't come into it. He'd be off Upstairs before anyone found out. But perhaps Marigold's parents wouldn't approve. There must be another solution.

That business about the midnight deadline sprang into his mind. What was the girl's name again? Cinderine? Cinderanna? Cinderella – that was it! And wasn't there something about a fairy godmother doing a bit of hocus-pocus with a pumpkin and a couple of mice? Surely he should be able to bring off a trick like that if he put his mind to it.

Pity he wasn't allowed to fly until he made it Upstairs. Some entrance to the gig that would be! He was really looking forward to the flying lessons he'd been promised as soon as his Upstairs passport was approved. Apparently, once they had your details on the database you were issued with wings and sent on an instruction course. Although he was incredibly sad to be leaving Marigold, (old softy that he'd become), there was a part of him that felt almost ready to be a full-time angel. Maybe the afterlife wouldn't be so awful after all.

As it grew dark, the weather changed. Summer had finally been invaded by autumn. Clouds shrouded the moon and a chill wind sneaked in from the north. The trees swayed, creaked, bent, their branches locking horns as a sudden storm blew in from the sea. A squall of stuttering rain lashed everything in its path, including the ghostly Luke. He wished he'd thought of bringing his old hoodie.

He shivered, his mind filled with sweet-and-sour thoughts. This half-life didn't have a lot going for it. The picture of his body lying in a fridge wrapped in a white sheet waiting to be identified gave him the creeps. Who would make the identification? Leslie, Helen, Danny? Most people who knew him well enough had departed from this world. He shrugged, not his problem. Now, he just wanted to get it over with.

Giving himself a mental shake, he rallied his forces. If this was to be his last night he'd better make it worthwhile. He glanced at his watch – almost time to make his final entrance into the girl's dreams. Tomorrow, he'd work out a way of getting to the gig in style. He squared his shoulders and slipped from his perch, sloughing off his earthbound personality before evaporating into the ether.

Once he'd checked that Marigold was sound asleep and dreaming, Luke went into boy-mode and tried to pick up where he'd left off. He slouched against an oak tree. 'OK there, Goldielocks?'

Marigold was thoroughly cheesed-off. Did Luke have to do the dream-thing tonight of all nights? She needed an uninterrupted night if she was to be bright and bushy-tailed for her big date. She watched him warily. Just as she thought, he was no longer the good-mannered student who had charmed her parents, more a layabout with penetrating eyes. 'I thought you'd given up this kind of thing.'

'Not to worry, this is my last time on dream duty.'

'Good.' She shuddered like a ghost had walked over her grave. It wasn't simply Luke's presence that made her uneasy. It was more a sensation of unfinished business. She couldn't shake it off. Something strange was niggling at her, demanding her attention. It wasn't the thunderstorm, the jagged lightning, the numbing rain, although all that was pretty scary. It was a feeling that tore at her heart.

She found herself taking moon-steps through tall wet grasses, not quite walking, not quite flying, typical dream-stuff. Luke lazily kept pace with her.

'Not so fast. You'll do yourself a mischief. You're no free-runner, that's for sure,' he said, grabbing her by the arm.

'Whatever.' She shrugged him off.

She stopped. Listened. There it was again. A sound she couldn't put a name to. In the teeth of the storm, with rain lashing down and the wind whipping branches to a frenzy, it was hard to make out where it was coming from - or who was causing it. She cupped a hand to her ear, willing herself to concentrate. *Listen!* She heard it again, the unmistakeable sound of a baby crying. Imagine a baby being caught up in the dream-thing - in a storm! Marigold *had* to find her, no matter what. With a half-memory of 'Hush-a-bye-baby' in her head, she moon-jumped high enough to peer into every tree top. No babies, just birds huddling in their nests, their tiny bird-nappies flapping on the topmost branches.

Marigold tossed and turned in her sleep, growing ever more agitated. She heard the baby's cries growing louder and more demanding. 'Help!' she called, but Luke had conveniently disappeared. I'll have to work this out on my own, she thought, so what's new?

She jumped over logs and fallen branches, over deep puddles and swollen streams. Nothing fazed her tonight. As she leapt into the air, she looked at her flying feet, surprised to see she was wearing one pink and one bright red shoe. Where had they come from?

At last she smelled the sea. Home territory. Good. She found herself on a bright blue cliff path. She didn't pause to query its blueness, simply acknowledging that it was the colour of Mum's favourite lustre jug, last seen filled with thick cream. The thought made her feel hungry. But she climbed on, pulled by some kind of cosmic rope until she reached the top and dared to look down. The wind was rising, waves pounded the rocks below, but the baby had gone quiet. Had she fallen over the edge?

She need not have worried. The boy was on the case. As suddenly as he had gone, he reappeared, pushed past her and reached into the void to catch the baby one-handed as it went flying through the air, its tiny mewling voice lost in the storm. He placed it gently into a gull's nest on the cliff-face.

Marigold found her voice. 'Hey, what do you think you're doing? That's my little sister you're throwing about!'

'Brother,' Luke said.

Marigold inched down the face of the cliff. She *had* to get hold of the baby, no matter what.

'Watch out!' the boy warned, but too late. Marigold lost her footing and felt herself falling, tumbling from rock to rock, towards the greedy waves. Everything happened in slow motion. She managed to grab the baby from the gull's nest as she fell. Then her shoes disappeared. First the red, then the pink one, fell from her feet and splashed into the sea. With the baby safe in her arms, she felt no fear, just incredibly sad for the pretty shoes.

There was an almighty crash. Then nothing.

'Easy, easy now. Good girl.' At long last she had stopped falling. She heard Luke's calm voice, felt cold sea-spray on her face. She found herself trussed up – in seaweed? grass? a life jacket? she didn't know. Whatever it was, it was surprisingly soft. She held the baby tight against her chest, Luke's arms around both of them. Struggling under his weight, she tried to cry out, but her voice wouldn't work properly. 'The baby,' she gasped. 'You're squashing her.'

'Him,' Luke said.

She came round slowly, opening her eyes to find herself on the bedroom floor, entangled in the duvet, rain on her face and wind in her hair. No baby. There was a strange half-light in the room. No dream this time, more a living nightmare. She was shivering with cold and a terrible sense of loss.

'The baby?'

'Not to worry, he's safe . . . My mum's looking after him – she's good with babies.' Luke's eyes had gone cold once more, icy blue as the Boy's. She had to look away. He rocked her in his arms, duvet and all as he attempted to protect her from the worst of the storm. She tried to work out what had happened. How come it was raining *inside* her bedroom?

'You'll be OK. I've got you,' he soothed.

'But what happened?'

'A tree's come down in the gale. Don't try to move.' He was terrified to think what *might* have happened. For once, he'd been in the right place at the right time.

When she was able to focus, she made out a huge tree lying across her pillow, its roots hanging from the window ledge. It had fallen exactly where she'd been sleeping a few minutes ago. Framed by flying curtains and shattered glass, its broken branches and wet leaves shivered in the wind. Marigold fought to free herself from the duvet, but Luke pinned her down.

'Not yet, not yet. There's glass all over the place,' he said. Then, in that uncanny way he had, he dissolved into the ether.

'My God, what's happened? Are you OK, Kid?' Dad flung open the door, taking over from the invisible Luke. 'Hold still. Don't try to move or you'll cut yourself.'

'I found the baby, Dad.'

'What baby?'

'Your baby, yours and Bunny's.'

'Shh,' Dad said, his eyes round with horror, as Mum appeared in the doorway. 'You've been dreaming. There *is* no baby, Kid. Got it?' Unable, for the moment, to unpick dream from reality, Marigold nodded in agreement. It was easier that way.

Mum wore Dad's ancient camel-hair dressing gown, tied like a sack around her waist, mermaid hair streaming down her back. 'That flaming old tree,' she said, clicking her tongue in exasperation, 'I told you, Oliver – you should have had it down years ago.' She ferreted around, torn between picking shards of glass off the duvet and having a go at Dad. He pretended he hadn't heard. Things were swiftly getting back to normal in Marigold's life.

'You must have a guardian angel, Kid.' Dad had never spoken a truer word. Marigold could imagine Luke's smirk of triumph. 'If you hadn't rolled out of bed and on to the floor, you'd be dead meat, for sure!'

'You couldn't get me out of this, could you?' Marigold asked. 'I feel like a mummy.'

'Don't be ridiculous! *I'm* the mummy in this house, don't you go forgetting it.' So nothing had changed there either. Mum was famous for getting hold of the wrong end of any stick.

'Keep your eyes closed, Kid. Hold this, Molly, and we'll have you out of there in no time.'

Once she had been released from the duvet, Marigold realised she must have come within an inch of being killed. On reflection, no, she certainly didn't want to die. She gave herself a mental talking-to. No more stuff about doing away with herself. There was a lot of living to be done and she was up for it.

Tonight was her big night – she hugged herself in anticipation – so it was all systems go. A shower, as hot as she could stand it, chased off any lingering demons – even the dream gradually lost its hold. But, no matter how hard she tried, she couldn't quite get rid of her sadness over the baby, her nearly half-sister. Luke's 'brother' echoed in her head. 'OK, brother then,' she said aloud. 'I can go along with that.' But the sad feeling stayed.

By the time she emerged, hair swathed in a towel, the Merrick team had swung into action. Dad organised a drinking mate with a tractor to haul the old tree into the garden and had nailed a polythene sheet over the broken window. Mum had produced gardening gloves and between them they'd cleared away every shard of broken glass from the carpet, from books and old toys. They even found a few pieces embedded in the dirty linen basket. The bedding was ditched wholesale into a bin bag.

'Time you got rid of that old Barbie stuff,' Mum said. 'I expect you'd like something a bit more sophisticated. We'll get it back on the insurance, won't we, Oliver?' Shades of the old days, Marigold thought, as her parents worked together and even managed a few mild jokes at one another's expense.

As soon as the sound of the vacuum died away and the last bin bag got rid of, Marigold, hopping with impatience, crept upstairs to check up on her clothes. For the very first time in her life, she found herself afflicted by the 'nothing to wear' syndrome. The skimpy tops looked too skimpy, the trendy skirts too trendy. Trousers were more her thing. She spent an hour looking through and rejecting every article of clothing she possessed. Finally she settled on the Bunny-inspired scarlet top, handkerchief skirt and a lacy shrug.

Next, she trawled through her shoes. Nothing doing. Unfortunately, Bunny's influence hadn't got as far as her feet. Trainers were out, so she was left with school shoes, (no way) or sandals, (kiddy-stuff.) As a trip to town wasn't on, she opted for tarting up the old white sandals by using Bunny's red nail varnish to paint a pattern on the toes. She'd seen it done on daytime TV. Hoping for the best, she left the sandals on a newspaper to dry. She worried about her hair, up or down? Earrings? A scarf? She couldn't stay still.

'You got ants in your pants or something?' her mother asked, as Marigold passed her on the stairs for the tenth time in the afternoon. 'If you've got nothing better to do, you could pop along to Spar for a dozen eggs and a brown loaf.'

The time between lunch and 8 o'clock seemed to stretch out taut as an elastic band. Marigold could almost hear it twanging. Her head was full of what-ifs and she was glad to have something useful to do. What if Luke didn't turn up? What if she didn't look the part? What if Luke disappeared mid-gig?

The Spar shop was busy. Everyone seemed to know what had happened to the Merricks and wanted to chat about her narrow escape. 'That's one of your nine lives gone,' the check-out girl said as she counted out her change.

An elderly woman standing behind her in the queue butted in. Marigold had never set eyes on her before, but she had an otherworldly look about her. She was very earnest. 'Trust me,' she whispered to the startled woman waiting behind her, 'that girl's got an angel on her shoulder.' Some angel, Marigold thought as two Mars bars suddenly appeared in her basket and Luke winked at her from behind the confectionery shelf. 'In case we get peckish later.'

Well, at least he's remembered, that's a plus. She went hot and cold when she thought of all the things that could go wrong and forced herself to take it slowly on the way home, counting paving slabs as she went. She took extreme care not to step on a crack, not that she believed in all that stuff, of course, but she wasn't taking any chances, not today, of all days. The rain had gone and a silvery sun lit up the road. A good omen for the evening ahead?

Her mobile trilled. Jocelyn. 'Who's the hot date?' she asked. 'You kept that well-hidden, didn't you?' She sounded pretty miffed. 'I thought I was supposed to be your BF?'

'You are.'

'You could have fooled me.'

True, Marigold hadn't mentioned going with Luke. It would be asking for trouble. She knew how totally unreliable he could be. What if, after all, he didn't turn up? She'd never live it down. 'I don't know what you mean,' she said.

'Don't give me all that guff – tonight, T-in-the-Park remember? News gets around.' But Jocelyn wasn't one to keep up the wronged friend front. 'What're you wearing?' Before Marigold could answer, she squeaked, 'Must dash – a text from Harry.' And she was off to work on her social life, all aggravation forgotten.

The afternoon ticked slowly past. Marigold picked up a book and threw it down unread. She experimented with some of Bunny's hair mousse and brushed it out again in disgust. She checked on her sandals. They still looked gross. Six o'clock rolled around at last.

'Aren't you coming down for something to eat?' her mother called from the kitchen, just as though it was any old night.

'I'm not hungry.'

'Nonsense! No child of mine goes out on an empty stomach, you should know that by now,' Mum said, in a tone you dare not argue with. Marigold had no choice. She dutifully sat at the table, tapping her fork in impatience, until her mother slipped a mushroom omelette on to the plate in front of her. In spite of the excitement fluttering in her stomach, she ate every last morsel – and enjoyed it.

'Thanks, Mum,' she said, dropping a kiss on the top of her mother's head as she passed her chair.

'Get away with you, girl!' Mum tried to sound cross, but a pleased smile hovered around her mouth. 'It's a really big night for you, isn't it? Imagine it, my baby going out on her first date! I can hardly believe it.'

When the door bell rang, Marigold was still struggling with her sandals. The nail varnish hadn't dried properly. She grabbed a bundle of tissues and scrubbed. It made them look even worse, if that were possible. Oh well, she thought, they'll have to do. I don't expect people will look at my feet much anyway.

Downstairs, Luke was charming the pants off her parents. To be sure, he had scrubbed up pretty well. He wore khaki jeans and a white tee-shirt with a chunky gold chain at the neck. His hair was gelled-up in the approved trendy style and he smelled of musky after-shave. He was the kind of young man any girl would be proud to be seen with.

There was just one problem. From his left hand swung two motorcycle helmets. Dead old-fashioned they were, like upturned black bowls. These did not bode well.

Marigold thought she'd covered every possible base, but motorbikes certainly hadn't featured anywhere in her imagination. I'll never be able to suss this guy out, even if he was going to be around for years which, of course, he's not. But she didn't want to think negative thoughts tonight. 'All set?' she asked.

But there was no way Dad was ready to let them go. He was hooked. He walked round and round the gleaming machine, all motorcycle gossip, style, make, age. 'A Honda, 1982, now that's quite something!' he enthused.

'The last air-cooled model,' Luke told him. Marigold couldn't care less. All she wanted was to be on her way, before this god-like creature disappeared in a puff of smoke.

'Dad, we'd better go. Don't want to be late.' Pointedly, she looked at her watch.

'Not to worry. We'll make it in loads of time, trust me.' Luke was in no mood to be hurried. She needn't have gone to all that trouble with her hair after all, she thought, as he plonked a helmet on her head and tucked her hair out of the way. He made sure the strap was fastened safely under her chin.

'Let's make tracks,' he said at last. He swung into his seat, twisting round to see if his passenger was settled. 'I forgot to say, you look smashing.' Unused to compliments, Marigold's face went bright red. Just as well Luke couldn't see it.

'Sure you can manage this thing?' she asked, a mite nervously.

'Course I can! Ready? Hold tight,' he said, as he revved the engine, and checked his mirrors. The machine roared into life and they turned into the road. All in all, Luke was pretty pleased with himself. The Honda wasn't a bad exchange for the abandoned supermarket trolley with two wheels missing he'd found on the council tip. Mice and a pumpkin were considered a bit old hat these days. Like most other things, magic had come into the 21st century.

It was the most exciting ride of Marigold's life. Houses and gardens, fences and trees flew past in a blur. She wouldn't have been surprised to find that they were actually airborne. But that was silly, silly – until she saw not only roofs and treetops, but tall wind turbines slide below their wheels, the supermarket at St Austell, the Trewithian roundabout.

All too soon, they swooped down on to the B3287 as signposts to the Lost Gardens came into sight. They joined the slow-moving queue for the car park. The attendant in his day-glow jacket directed them to an appropriate slot. His eyes didn't even flicker. To him it must have looked like any other common-or-garden motorbike, nothing special. Maybe it was her heated imagination. Perhaps they hadn't been flying after all. Luke trundled the bike into its space. He removed his helmet and ran fingers through his hair, spiking it up so it looked as good as new.

'We flew that last bit, didn't we?'

Luke gave her one of his old-fashioned looks, his eyes cold, like they were back in the dream-thing. 'I couldn't possibly say.' She'd almost forgotten how maddening he could be.

They were drawn into the crowd surging through the gates. Heligan was always an exciting place to be, but tonight was something else. There were lights in the trees and glow-sticks edged the paths. Luke and Marigold joined the hordes of hyped-up kids jostling their way to the Flora's Green. As they heard bands checking their sound gear, the febrile atmosphere ratcheted up another notch. The staid daytime park, surrounded as it was by a ring of fairy-lit rhododendrons, was unrecognisable. Noise from the sound system reverberated through the trees and spotlights glitzed the darkening sky. Marigold, breathless with high octane excitement, could scarcely hear herself speak.

Luke reached for her hand, 'Got something for you,' he said, producing an orange plastic bag. 'Go on, open it before we get swept away.'

Shoes, neat little pumps, one red, one pink. They fitted perfectly. 'How did you know my size?' she asked.

'An educated guess.' Marigold dropped her old sandals into the garbage bin, only too pleased to see them disappear.

'Nice,' she said, wondering if anyone would notice they didn't match. 'Thank you.' Her hand in Luke's grew clammy with heat and sweat, but she wasn't about to let go. If this is what the boy-girl thing does for you, I'm all for it, she thought.

'Like a Smoothie before it gets going?' Luke asked. 'Cranberry OK?' Cranberry, her favourite flavour. How did he get things so right? He produced the Mars bars from his pocket. A posse of Year 8 boys slouched against the Smoothie stall. They whistled and nudged one another.

'Look what Fatso's bagged!' Kevin said, in his usual role as ringleader.

'Come on, Kev, she's not a bad-looking bird these days,' his best mate ventured.

'You gone soft in the head, have you?' This was bravado. Kevin could have kicked himself. This Mark 2 version of Marigold Merrick was quite something and now this jumped-up blond bloke had succeeded where he had failed. As they melted into the crowd, he felt positively venomous towards Luke, who treated him to one of his drop-dead looks. Pity the cops were so slow in following up his story about the poster. But he had him in his sights. He'd get him yet.

Luke and Marigold wandered round the stalls as they waited for the concert proper to begin. At the burger bar, they bumped into Jocelyn who did a double-take when she saw Luke close-to. 'Now, that's what I call fit!' she managed in a stage-whisper, above the sound of the warm-up. 'No wonder you kept him under wraps.' For once, Marigold had upstaged her in the boyfriend department.

When Harry came back with their burgers, Jocelyn thought how uncool he looked compared to Marigold's Luke. Her fallback response to any half-decent guy was to flirt a bit, so she flashed her eyes at Luke, but he wasn't having any of it. Be like that, she thought, hurrying Harry off to find their seats. Not that anyone had any intention of sitting down, of course.

There was a lull as the first of the boy-bands took to the stage, then screams, louder and louder, as the beat took hold and the lead-singer of the *Bo-Jangles* grabbed a mike by its throat and all but made love to it.

The evening passed in a blur of whooping and screaming. As the noise rose to a crescendo and the atmosphere grew hot and sweaty, Marigold found herself yelling along with the best of them. She screamed until her throat turned raw, unable to believe the sounds coming out of her mouth. It was as though a monster had taken over the entire audience.

As one great beast, they jumped to the beat and bellowed in frenzy – all except Luke, who managed to remain above it all, almost austere. He squeezed Marigold's hand from time to time, pleased that she was enjoying herself. He was astonished to see how abandoned she'd become. She radiated an unholy joy, like she'd been lit up from the inside. This was an entirely different girl from the one he thought he knew. Even her mother would be pushed to recognise her tonight, he thought.

But, no matter how hard Luke tried, he couldn't relax. He felt uninvolved, an outsider, a mere spectator. The incredible noise began to get to him and fill his head with a nagging pain. Despite the sweated air swirling round the Green, he felt his body heat begin to leak out. He held his free hand up to the spotlight. As he had suspected, the bones were starting to show through. With a lump in his throat, he realised his time had come – earlier than he'd reckoned.

'Marigold,' he said. No response, she didn't have a chance of hearing him over the ear-splitting music. She was completely carried away by the five young men gyrating on stage to the hypnotic beat. 'Goldielocks!' This time, his voice was louder, more urgent. He pulled on her hand.

'What's wrong?'

'We've got to go.'

'Don't be ridiculous. The second set's just started.'

'Well, five minutes or so, no more.' She barely glanced in his direction.

'Loosen up for pity's sake!' she said, and for a brief moment tore her eyes away from the lights and really looked at Luke. He was standing by her side, stiff as a tree trunk. Everyone else in the crowd was moving, hands aloft, twisting their bodies to the music, sinuous as eels in running water. 'Give it a go, can't you.'

'We haven't got long. I promised your dad I'd bring you back safe and sound.' If he was to get her home before midnight, Honda or no Honda, they'd have to get a move on. The noise was escalating. Girls were shrieking at the tops of their voices, lads whistling and cheering. Lights danced over the swirling crowd, painting them blue, gold, green.

'Don't let's go, not yet. I'm having such a fabulous time,' Marigold panted. Her hair was matted round her face, mascara making tracks on her cheeks. She was a girl in a trance.

'Now!' Luke said. He began to drag her away.

'But Luke . . .' She was on the point of crying with disappointment as he hauled her, none too gently, to the edges of the throng. 'Let me go!' She tried to squirm out of his grasp. No-one took any notice. They were too consumed by the music to bother with a couple of kids falling out.

Once out of the spotlights, Marigold saw for herself that Luke was fading. He was becoming the guy in the dream-thing, no more than a shadow. This was serious, so she tried to get her head together. 'You're not thinking of disappearing are you? Not now, not here.' She felt the first frisson of fear.

Pushing with difficulty through the frenzied crowd on the Green, they made their way back to the car-park. She could have sworn they'd parked the motorbike in Bay C4, but it was nowhere to be seen. In its place was a battered shopping trolley with two cycle helmets placed neatly in the basket.

'Damn and blast! We've left it too late. I'm sorry, Goldielocks.' Luke kicked the trolley and it rolled sadly into the hedge. 'Upstairs have got their wires crossed. I'm sure they said midnight and there's still an hour to go.' And then he said a very bad word, one that should not have fallen from the lips of a angel, no matter what the circumstances. Marigold tried to smile. 'Perhaps they won't let you in.'

'No such luck. They've got my papers ready and waiting.' Away from the hysteria of the concert, in the lee of the shadowy hedge, Luke put his fingers under Marigold's chin and turned her face towards him. He badly wanted to kiss her. He pulled the gold chain from his neck. 'Here, take this,' he whispered.

'I can't. It suits you. You'll want it again.'

'Not where I'm going, I won't. I don't think it would go too well with a pair of wings, do you?'

Marigold took a step back. 'You're going for good this time? Really truly?'

'No choice.' Luke's complexion was almost luminous in the thin moonlight. 'This is it, Goldielocks.' She felt a cold kiss, like a frosted leaf, flutter against her lips. 'Think of it this way, no more dream-thing, I promise.' And, before her eyes, he faded into the night.

'Luke!' she called. 'Luke! Come back!'

'I can't, my love, I'm sorry. You know that, don't you?' His voice was a mere echo of itself, coming from the middle of the hedge somewhere. 'That baby brother of yours needs me. I can hear him crying.'

'Sister.'

'Brother, I told you.' Even now he was ready to argue the toss. Marigold found herself standing alone in the car park. She tried to fasten Luke's chain round her neck, checking with her fingertips to see if it was real. She wouldn't have been a bit surprised if it had dissolved along with Luke himself. 'Here, let me.' She felt cold fingertips on her neck. 'Job done, Goldielocks. Gotta go.'

Away from the heat and excitement of the crowd, she shivered. She tugged her cobwebby shrug around her, unsure of what to do next. She'd never felt so sad.

'Buck up, Goldielocks. Look out for Kevin's friend, Dave. He fancies you rotten.'

'How do you know?'

'I have an ear for gossip, but in a good way. Dave will be only too delighted to see you home, trust me.' Luke's voice was no more than a whisper now, a breeze shivering in the treetops. She could just make out his words, but of Luke himself, there was no sign. 'Not to worry, Goldielocks, you're not on your own. I'll stick around till Dave takes over.' She looked up to see where the voice was coming from and ducked as a white owl swooped low over her head. It flew to a branch on the edge of the path and winked a round yellow eye at her. Luke's idea of a joke, she decided – and a great improvement on the white cow.

As Marigold stumbled back towards the crowd, drawn by the thumping beat, a familiar figure came towards her. 'Did that guy stand you up? I thought he might.' Just as Luke had promised, Dave appeared alongside and tentatively took her arm. She squinted up at him. In the half-dark, he *was* reasonably good-looking. 'Cold?' he asked and placed his sweater round her shoulders. 'Fancy taking in the last set with me?'

She nodded. What was it her mother said? No use crying over spilt milk. She knew she had no choice. She'd never see Luke again, certainly not in this life. But, she could do worse than Dave, she thought, glancing to catch him sizing her up – almost as though he'd lost a penny and found a pound. 'I've got my Dad's car tonight. Can I take you home?'

'Thanks.'

He caught sight of Marigold's feet. 'What's with the odd shoes?' he asked. 'Fall out of bed, did you?'

'No,' she said. 'It's a girl thing. It'll soon be all the rage – you watch!'

She linked her fingers in his and allowed Dave to lead her back into the crowd. The music was still throbbing, the girls still screaming, the lads whistling louder than ever. There was still another hour to go.

And, what's more, Marigold thought, I'm going back to the gig with a real-live boy this time, one who fancies me rotten. Then, almost drowned out by the music, she heard the eerie sound of an owl hooting as it took off into the night.